"Hey Wanda,"  *"while you're up, how about frying a few slices of bacon for me? Thanks."*

Wanda didn't get the bacon right away. Instead, she filled a teakettle with water, placed it on the stove, then turned on the bluish gas flame. Then she turned to the counter to get a mug and a spoon.

Wheeeeeeee!!!

The shrill shriek of a whistle pierced Wishbone's ears.

Wanda stared at the kettle with disbelief.

"Is your water boiling already?" Joe called over the harsh whistling. "Didn't you just put it on?

"Just . . . just . . . just this very m-moment," Wanda stammered.

Joe went to the mug. "This is impossible. Water can't boil that fast." Joe stuck a finger in the mug, then quickly pulled it out. "Ouch! It's boiling, all right."

Wanda looked around the kitchen with helpless confusion. "Something weird is happening in Hathaway House!"

WISHBONE SUPER Mysteries

THE HAUNTING OF HATHAWAY HOUSE

by Alexander Steele
WISHBONE™ created by Rick Duffield

Big Red Chair Books™, *A Division of **Lyrick Publishing**™*

This book is a work of fiction. The characters, incidents, and dialogues are products of the author's imagination and are not to be construed as real. Any resemblance to actual events or persons, living or dead, is entirely coincidental.

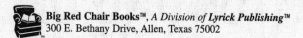 **Big Red Chair Books**™, *A Division of **Lyrick Publishing**™*
300 E. Bethany Drive, Allen, Texas 75002

©1999 Big Feats Entertainment, L.P.

Edited by Kevin Ryan

Copy edited by Jonathon Brodman

Continuity editing by Grace Gantt

Cover design/photo illustration by Lyle Miller

Interior illustrations by Al Fiorentino

Wishbone photograph by Carol Kaelson

Library of Congress Catalog Card Number: 99-61518

ISBN: 1-57064-590-6

First printing: October 1999

10 9 8 7 6 5 4 3 2 1

Printed in the United States of America

To Kerry, who always listens,
with her eyes as wide as saucers

FROM THE BIG RED CHAIR . . .

Oh . . . hi! Wishbone here. You caught me right in the middle of some of my favorite things—books. Let me welcome you to THE WISHBONE SUPER MYSTERIES. In each story, I help my human friends solve a puzzling mystery. In *THE HAUNTING OF HATHAWAY HOUSE*, my neighbor, Wanda Gilmore, inherits an old house rumored to be haunted. My pals—Joe, David, and Sam—and I quickly agree to join her to check it out. We're off to a great start, until Wanda unlocks the front door. . . .

This story takes place in the fall, during the same time period as the events that you'll see in the second season of my WISHBONE® television show. In this story, Joe is fifteen, and he and his friends are in the ninth grade. Like me, they are always ready for adventure . . . and a good mystery.

You're in for a real treat, so pull up a chair, grab a snack, and sink your teeth into *THE HAUNTING OF HATHAWAY HOUSE!*

Chapter One

Wishbone stopped dead in his tracks, his tail standing up stiffly.

A ghost floated in a window of the Hernandez house.

Am I seeing what I think I'm seeing? the white-with-brown-and-black-spots Jack Russell terrier wondered. *Maybe I should check it out. On the other paw, maybe I shouldn't. But the good people of Oakdale depend on me to watch out for their safety. Hey, I'm a watchdog, not a chicken!*

The dog crept forward—slowly, carefully, keeping his trim body low to the ground. When he entered the Hernandez yard, however, he discovered that the "ghost" wasn't really a ghost. It was just a piece of cardboard, cut and painted to look like a ghost.

Wishbone glanced around to make sure nobody was watching. *Okay, false alarm. Since no one saw me, this can just be my little secret. No sense in ruining my reputation for fearlessness. But why was there a . . . Oh, yes, of course. It's only three days away from Halloween!*

7

Wishbone loved holidays. At Thanksgiving, he gave thanks for roasted turkey, bread-crumb dressing, and cranberry sauce. At Christmas, he merrily made his way to all sorts of parties that served all sorts of merry food. On the Fourth of July, he celebrated his independence by begging for hot dogs at the town picnic. And Halloween, of course, meant lots and lots of candy treats.

The dog walked along the circular cul-de-sac where his home was. It was a crisp, clear blue afternoon in late October. Autumn leaves crackled beneath the dog's paws as if they were ancient scraps of paper.

Wishbone paused. His nose picked up the slightly sweet smell of pumpkin in the area. Figuring there might be a pumpkin pie in the making, he followed the scent. After going a short distance, Wishbone found himself at the back of a house that belonged to his next-door neighbor, Wanda Gilmore.

Wishbone scratched at the back door with his front paws. "Helllooo! Wanda, it's me! Your friendly neighbor, Wishbone!"

No one answered, even though Wishbone heard voices inside.

"Come on, Wanda, let me in! I came over just to pay you a nice, neighborly visit!"

Still, there was no answer.

Wishbone scratched at the door, much harder this time. "Hey, Wanda, open up! You know I can't resist a freshly baked pumpkin pie!"

Finally, Wanda opened the door.

Wanda Gilmore was one of a kind. She was a slender woman with short auburn hair and very distinct features. Wanda had an offbeat personality, lots of interesting moods, and a very lively taste in clothing. At the moment, she was wearing striped pants, a paisley-patterned vest, and some kind of weird headband.

On the good side, Wanda was interested in all kinds of things, including gardening, history, local politics, literature, and spending time with kids. On the down side, she had a big problem with Wishbone digging in her flower beds.

"Wishbone," Wanda said, glancing around the yard, "you haven't been digging in my garden, have you?"

"No, I wasn't digging in the garden," Wishbone insisted. "I was calling and calling to get you to open the door. That's probably the *last thing* I would do if I was digging in the garden. So . . . let's have a look at that pie."

Wishbone figured Wanda was still suspicious about the digging, because she pretended she hadn't heard a word he said.

Okay, so don't listen to the dog, Wishbone thought, trotting into Wanda's kitchen. *Sometimes it seems that nobody listens to me around here. Oh, well, they don't know what they're missing.*

Wishbone saw Samantha Kepler, nicknamed Sam, sitting at the kitchen table. "Hi, Wishbone," she said, leaning over to stroke the dog's fur.

When Sam gave Wishbone a scratch or pat, the dog knew he was in good hands. Sam was generous to everyone, whether they were human, dog, or otherwise. She also excelled at doing things requiring artistic talent, whether it was drawing, decorating, or her favorite hobby, photography.

Sam's silky blond hair framed her hazel eyes. But Sam did not spend a lot of time fussing over how she

looked. She often wore her hair simply pulled back into a ponytail.

Wishbone had been noticing that Sam wore her hair in a ponytail less and less lately. Wishbone wondered if it was because Sam had recently begun the ninth grade at Wilson High School. The dog thought his friend might be trying out a more grown-up look.

Wanda joined Sam at the table. Wishbone noticed that they were carving faces into plump pumpkins with sharp knives. Wanda's pumpkin wore a scary frown, and Sam's pumpkin showed an even scarier smile. A nearby collection of untouched pumpkins waited patiently for their make-overs.

So they're not fixing mouth-watering pumpkin pie, Wishbone thought with disappointment. *They're carving jack-o'-lanterns. Those are no good to eat. At least I don't think they are.*

There was a knock at the back door. Then Joe Talbot

and David Barnes stepped into the kitchen. Like Sam, the two boys had also begun the ninth grade at Wilson High.

"Hello, Miss Gilmore. How's it going, Sam?" Joe said with a wave.

Wishbone had lived with Joe since his puppy days. Friendly and dependable, Joe Talbot was the kind of boy who earned humans the title of "Dog's Best Friend." He had straight brown hair, which often fell across his forehead, no matter how much he pushed it back. A talented athlete, Joe was a starter on the Wilson High junior-varsity basketball team.

"This place looks like a jack-o'-lantern factory," David said.

David Barnes lived right next door to Joe and Wishbone. He had dark, curly hair and intense eyes that seemed to take in everything around him. He was an expert at doing almost anything of a scientific or mechanical nature. So he spent a lot of time doing experiments in his super-cool garage laboratory. David also knew about computers the way a dog knew about bones.

Wishbone, Joe, Sam, and David had been best friends with one another as long as Wishbone could remember. Together they had experienced countless adventures, and the dog liked to think of them as a perfectly matched pack.

"Pull up a pumpkin and join us," Sam said with a warm smile.

"No, thanks," Joe replied. "We just wanted to stop by and say hi. We're on our way to David's house. He's going to show me this new Web site he's building."

"It's for Snook's Furniture store," David said proudly. "My first professional assignment."

"Congratulations!" Wanda said, clapping her hands a few times. "But I still think you boys ought to carve some pumpkins with us. This Halloween, I'm planning to have jack-o'-lanterns glowing all over the house and in the front yard. It'll be so creepy. Come on, it'll help you get into the Halloween spirit!"

"Miss Gilmore," Joe said, making a face, "we're in high school now."

"What's that supposed to mean?" Wanda asked.

"Once you get to a certain age," David explained, "candy isn't so important anymore. All of that Halloween stuff . . . well, it loses its scary factor."

"Candy becomes less important?" Wishbone said with disbelief. "What are you talking about?"

Sam looked a little sadly at her jack-o'-lantern's jagged smile. "David's right. It takes a lot more than a hollowed-out pumpkin with a candle glowing inside to give us a scare."

Oh, I see. So the kids think they've gotten too big for a little "trick or treat."

Sam heard three knocks at Wanda's front door.

"Ah, that must be Mr. Whipple," Wanda said, jumping from her chair.

"Who's Mr. Whipple?" David asked.

"I'm not quite sure," Wanda said, wiping her hands on a hand towel. "He's an attorney from New Hampshire. He called a few days ago to say he wanted to see me this afternoon."

Wanda walked through the dining room, passed through the strings of hanging glass beads, then entered the living room. Sam and the others followed close behind. Sam was eager to see why this visitor from New Hampshire had come by. She figured it had to be about something interesting. In the life of Wanda Gilmore, Sam knew, there was seldom a dull moment.

Wanda opened the front door. An elderly man stood facing her. He held a briefcase in one hand, a fedora hat in the other.

Sam thought the man looked very formal and proper, although she noticed there was a lively twinkle in his deep blue eyes. Underneath a topcoat that was open, he wore an elegant-looking suit, set off by a perfectly tied bow tie. He had a moustache, and his neatly combed hair shined as white as freshly fallen snow. The man seemed well over seventy years of age.

"Hello," the man said politely. "Are you Wanda Gilmore?"

"Yes," Wanda replied. "And you must be—"

The man gave a slight bow of his head. "Oliver Matheson Whipple the Third."

"Well, please come in," Wanda said, showing the man inside. "Have a seat. Would you like something to drink?"

"No, thank you," Mr. Whipple said, as Wanda took his hat and coat.

Mr. Whipple seemed puzzled by the decor of the living room, which was the opposite of formal and proper. The room held bizarre-looking furniture, eye-popping clashes of color, and very modern artwork, some of it made by Wanda herself.

13

"Everybody," Wanda announced, "meet Oliver Matheson Whipple the Third. Mr. Whipple, this is Joe, Sam, David, and the furry fellow is Joe's dog, Wishbone. None of them belongs to me, but they're all very good friends of mine."

"It's a pleasure," Mr. Whipple said, taking a seat in an armchair.

The others sat down, too. They all seemed curious about the man's visit.

"You have such an interesting name," Sam commented.

"Yes, I suppose it is," Whipple replied. "I am a descendant of William Whipple, one of the signers of the Declaration of Independence. He was a congressman from my home state of New Hampshire."

"I'm really curious to know why you're here," Wanda said, leaning forward in her chair.

Mr. Whipple folded his hands in his lap, his expression becoming serious. "I had some other business to take care of in this state. Anyway, I prefer to do this kind of thing in person. These situations can be rather upsetting. I thought a face-to-face meeting with you would be better than just contacting you by telephone or mail. And, heaven forbid, I would never communicate through this new e-mail system everyone is so crazy about."

Wanda looked worried. "You have upsetting news? What is it?"

"You have a cousin on your mother's side of your family by the name of Homer Hathaway. If I am not mistaken, he is the youngest son of your grandmother's youngest brother."

"Yes, that's correct. I met Homer Hathaway only

once, though. It was back when I was just a little girl. He must be . . . not so young anymore."

"He is eighty-four, to be exact. Or, to be *very* exact, he *was* eighty-four. Just last week, he passed away."

"Oh, dear. That's definitely not good news."

"No," Whipple said with a sigh, "but it's not such bad news, either. Homer Hathaway lived a long and happy life. And he died while doing something he truly loved. He was sailing in the sunlit waters just off the coast of Greece. An unexpected storm blew in from out at sea, with winds up to fifty knots. His boat sank and, well . . . that was the end of Homer Hathaway."

"I see. Thank you for telling me in person," Wanda said slowly.

"As an attorney," Whipple said with a hint of pride, "I try to be sensitive to the human side of things. Besides, I haven't come only to deliver the bad news. There is also some good news attached."

Wanda looked curious. "What would that be?"

"Homer Hathaway did not have any close relatives," Mr. Whipple explained. "His wife died many years ago. They had no children. The Hathaway family seems to have reduced greatly in number."

"Maybe Miss Gilmore has inherited some money," Joe whispered to David.

David nodded.

For some reason, Wishbone had raised his ears high.

With a faint smile, Whipple said, "Homer Hathaway left his small savings to charity. However . . . he did have a rather nice old house in Endicott, New Hampshire. And he wrote in his will that the house should be left to you, Miss Gilmore."

"To me?" Wanda said, raising her eyebrows.

Sam could see that she had been right—yet another interesting chapter in Wanda's life was unfolding.

"The house has always belonged to different members of the Hathaway family," Whipple explained. "Indeed, it is known as Hathaway House. And Homer very much wanted the house to *remain* in the family. It was between you, Miss Gilmore, and three or four other distant relatives. Even though you will be the first owner of the house whose last name isn't Hathaway, Homer thought you would be the best choice. He remembered what a spirited and spunky little girl you were. And it looks as if you have grown into a spirited and spunky woman."

Mr. Whipple's eyes took in the unusual decor of Wanda's house.

"I have a vague memory of Hathaway House," Wanda said, gazing into the distance. "I stayed there once with my family. As I recall, it was a wonderful old place."

"Miss Gilmore," Sam said, a little worried, "you wouldn't leave Oakdale, would you?"

"No, I won't be leaving Oakdale," Wanda assured Sam and the others. "But maybe I could use the New Hampshire house as a home away from home. It's very pretty around that area. Uh . . . would that be all right, Mr. Whipple?"

"If you accept the house," Whipple stated, "you may do with it as you wish. However, you don't have to make an immediate decision about the house. In fact, to be exact, you are not allowed to make an immediate decision."

"I'm not?"

"You see, there is one condition to the will. Homer suggested that you spend at least three nights in the house before you decide whether or not you would like to accept it. That way, you'll know exactly what you're getting."

"Of course," Wanda said, nodding. "That's a wise idea. When can I see it? As far as I'm concerned, the sooner the better."

"Sooner is also better for me," Whipple agreed. "Should you decide *not* to keep the house, I will have to move on to the next relative on the list."

"Could I go there tomorrow?" Wanda said eagerly. "Oh, I'm sorry if I'm getting too excited. It doesn't seem proper, considering that cousin Homer just passed away."

"On the contrary," Whipple pointed out, "Homer would be happy that you are happy. He was a happy man. I see no reason why you can't visit the house tomorrow."

"Was Homer a close friend of yours?" Wanda asked.

"Yes, indeed. We grew up together, and we were always very close."

"I am truly sorry about your loss."

"Yes, thank you," Mr. Whipple said, as he opened his briefcase and pulled out a manila envelope. "Now take this package, Miss Gilmore. Inside you will find house keys, a map and directions for getting to the house, and some other information. You'll also find a check to cover at least some of your travel expenses."

"Thank you," Wanda said, taking the envelope.

Whipple closed his briefcase, snapped it shut, then set it on the floor. "Miss Gilmore, there is one little detail that I should probably mention. For many years, there have been rumors that Hathaway House is haunted. Homer himself believed this to be true. However, I have been in that house many times, and I feel fairly certain

the rumors are nonsense. Nevertheless, I felt the need to mention it."

Sam felt her heartbeat quicken. She had never seen a ghost, and she really hadn't given them much thought. All the same, the word *haunted* never failed to give her a strange feeling of excitement.

Sam noticed David looking doubtfully at Joe. She knew the boys believed in ghosts even less than she did.

"Miss Gilmore," Sam said, looking at Wanda eagerly, "do you want someone to stay with you at the house?"

"Ah, yes, good idea," Wanda said, nodding. "But who could I get—"

"I'll go!" Sam said quickly. "It would be a fun trip."

"Me, too," David said. "I've always wanted to see that part of New England."

"Count me in," Joe added.

Even Wishbone looked longingly at Wanda.

Once the idea was out, it quickly caught fire among the kids.

"If we leave tomorrow and spend three nights there," David said in a rush of words, "we'll only miss Friday and Monday at school. I'm sure our parents will allow us to go."

"But you'll miss having Halloween in Oakdale," Wanda said.

"No big deal," Joe blurted out.

Wanda rubbed her chin. "I doubt that any of your parents could go. Joe, your mom is running the Halloween party at the library. David, your parents are going to help out at the party. And I know Halloween is a big night for Sam's dad at the pizza parlor. But maybe all of your parents will trust you kids in my—"

"They'll say yes," Sam said with confidence. "At least I think they will."

Sam was very eager to go with Wanda to Hathaway House. High-school life seemed to be moving faster than middle-school life, and Sam had been feeling a bit overwhelmed lately. She thought taking a trip to a mysterious place would be the perfect way to take a break from the pressure at school.

Wanda turned to Mr. Whipple. "Would it be all right if I brought some house guests?"

"Oh, absolutely," Whipple replied. "There are plenty of bedrooms."

"Will anyone be there to greet me?" Wanda asked.

Whipple pulled out a business card. "I'm afraid not. But here is my card. I won't be in my office next week. But if you call the number on my card and leave a message with any questions, I will get back to you as soon as possible. Also, I would appreciate receiving a call after your stay at Hathaway House. You can let me know if you intend to keep the house or not."

"And I need to stay there for three nights?" Wanda said, taking the card.

Mr. Whipple fixed his deep blue eyes on Wanda. "Homer recommended that you stay at least three nights. If you wish to stay for less time, Oliver Matheson Whipple will not argue with your decision. After all, Miss Gilmore, it is you who will be testing the house. The house will not be testing you."

Something about that last remark gave Sam a slight case of the creeps.

Chapter Two

Gazing out the car window, Wishbone watched the morning scenery fly by at fifty-five miles an hour. The dog loved adventurous trips, and this was his first journey to the part of the U.S.A. known as New England.

"O," Joe said.

"U," David said.

The kids were playing Ghost, a road-trip game that Wishbone had watched them play before. Each player would add a letter, trying to form a word. But the players had to be careful not to let a word end while it was their turn. If it did, that player would lose a point.

Wishbone was seated in the backseat of a rental car, right between Sam and David. Up front, Wanda was driving. Joe sat next to her, holding the map given to Wanda by Mr. Whipple.

The previous day, Joe, Sam, and David had each gotten permission from their parents to go with Wanda to the house she had inherited. Wishbone, of course, had insisted that he go on the trip, too. Just an hour before, the whole group had flown into the Boston airport. There, Wanda had rented a car. They were now traveling along an interstate highway, nearing their destination of Endicott, New Hampshire.

"I," Sam said.

"O-U-I?" David said, puzzled. "If you mean *oui*, that's the French word for *yes*. Foreign words aren't allowed."

"I'm not thinking of *oui*," Sam said with a sly smile.

"Well, I can't think of another word that starts with O-U-I," David said.

"Neither can I," Joe said.

"Ouija!" Sam said proudly. "You know, a Ouija board is one of the ways a ghostly spirit helps you find answers to questions. Since you guys couldn't think of the word, that's one point against each of you."

This girl seems to have ghosts on her mind, Wishbone thought, glancing at Sam. *I hope she's not counting on this house really being haunted. If so, she's probably headed for a big disappointment. Then, again, maybe . . .*

"Oh, just look at the lovely fall foliage!" Wanda cried with excitement. "There are no two ways about it. New England has the most beautiful autumns!"

Wishbone agreed completely. The leaves on the trees reminded him of a bowl overflowing with colorfully wrapped candy. Bursting orange, gleaming gold, sunshine yellow, flaming red, deep purple, and many other shades blended together in a way that almost made Wishbone's mouth water.

The weather, however, looked a bit threatening. Grayness tinted the sky, and Wishbone sensed that some bad weather might soon be headed for this area. It was also colder there than it had been in Oakdale.

"Oh, Miss Gilmore, could you slow down a sec?" Sam said, rolling down her window.

As Wanda slowed the car, Sam stuck her camera out the window, focused, then snapped a few shots. Sam's flowing blond hair blew loosely in the breeze.

The views were so eye-appealing that the miles and the time seemed to pass with great speed. Soon Wishbone saw a sign whiz by.

"That sign said 'Endicott,'" Joe said, checking his map. "We should turn off at the very next exit."

"Kids, there's so much history in this area," Wanda said with enthusiasm. "Of course, you know that Native Americans once lived here. And English settlers moved into these parts soon after the Pilgrims made their landing at Plymouth Rock. And some of the biggest battles of the Revolutionary War were fought right around here. And then, of course—"

"Exit!" Joe called out.

Still talking, Wanda exited off the highway and then drove along a narrow country road. Through the brilliantly colored trees, Wishbone glimpsed patches of distant blue, which he knew was the Atlantic Ocean.

The group saw nothing but trees for a while. Then houses began to appear alongside the road. They were all built in a similar style. Their siding was covered by flat wooden boards. Each house was painted a different color, but the colors were not as brilliant as those of the passing tree leaves.

"Don't you love these New England homes?" Wanda said. "That style there is called 'clapboard.' They've been building houses that way for a very long time around here."

"This is Wycliff Road," Joe said, studying his map. "Take a left."

Wanda turned onto a winding dirt road. Its uneven surface made the car bump and sway a bit. As the trees thinned out, an ocean bay came into view. The bay was a body of gentle blue water surrounded by a U-shape of rocky shoreline. In the distance, scattered houses looked down on the ocean from the shore's rising slopes. Floating on the water was a single sailboat, seeming no bigger than a child's toy.

"That should be it over there," Joe said, pointing.

The gray shape of a house came into view. It stood upon a hill of dead grass from where it overlooked the bay. There were no other houses nearby. This had to be Hathaway House.

Wanda turned the car into a gravel driveway that led to a closed garage. She parked the car, and everyone climbed out. The group hurried around to the front of the house, the side facing the ocean.

"Let's see what sort of property we've got on our paws," Wishbone said eagerly.

The dog looked up, examining the house carefully. The three-story house was shaped very much like a big square box. It was covered with horizontal boards of flat wood, in the style Wanda had called "clapboard." The boards were painted a light gray. But much of the paint was peeling, making the house seem worn down by the passing of time.

Wanda held her hands to her cheeks. "Oh, my, what a fabulous old house!"

"*Old* is right," David said, moving toward a small plaque on the house. "Look at this plaque. It says,

'Hathaway House. Built by Josiah Hathaway, Shipmaster-Merchant, in 1819.'"

"I guess Josiah Hathaway was a pretty important person in the shipping business," Joe said. "That's probably why he built such a big house right by the ocean."

Wishbone noticed something odd about the front of the house. It seemed to have a face.

On the first floor, a black front door and two windows with black shutters formed sort of a mouth. On the second floor, a three-sided bay window stuck out, almost like a nose. On the top floor, two smaller windows peeked out of little wooden units in the roof, almost like two eyes. A chimney shot upward on each side of the house. Wishbone wasn't sure if they looked more like ears or the horns of a devil.

Sam snapped a picture, then said, "I love those little windows that come out of the roof."

"Those are called gables," Wanda explained. "A gable is an architectural feature that has a window and extends out from the main beam of the roof. You see them a lot in New England architecture."

Wishbone looked at the surrounding area. The house stood on a hill covered with scrubby grass, which had already turned a yellow-brown because of the beginning of the cold season. The hill sloped gently down to the bay. There the land was met by a shore of pebbly sand and rocky outcroppings. Surrounding the house, snakelike weeds and vines lay sprawled across the ground. Some of them climbed the lower part of the house.

"Maybe I could plant a nice flower garden right there by the front porch," Wanda said, as if picturing it in her mind. "I wonder how rich the soil is around here."

"I'd be more than happy to test it out for you," Wishbone said. He immediately put his front paws into energetic motion.

The dog stopped his soil-sampling when Wanda gave him a sharp look.

"Come on, everyone," Wanda told the group, "I can't wait to get a look inside!"

They climbed some steps and came to a wooden porch that ran the length of the front of the house. From her purse, Wanda took a key, which she inserted in the lock. She gave the key a turn, then gripped the doorknob. With a creepy creak, the door opened.

Everyone stepped inside Hathaway House.

The air was chilly, and all sorts of unfamiliar smells drifted into Wishbone's nose. Wishbone and the rest of the group were standing in a long, narrow entrance hall. Rooms were to the left and right. Thin beams of sunlight filtered into the house, creating an odd mixture of both shadow and light. This was because the windows were covered by inside shutters that were closed almost all of the way.

Suddenly Wishbone noticed a group of white ghosts floating through the air.

"Ghosts!" Wishbone shouted, running wildly in a circle. "Ghosts everywhere! Quick, let's head for the hills!"

Joe knelt down and placed his hand on the dog's back. "It's okay, Wishbone. What are you so upset about, boy?"

As Joe rubbed Wishbone's back, the dog took another look at the place. This time he saw that the ghosts were really just white sheets draped over all the furniture.

"Uh . . . upset?" Wishbone said, slightly embarrassed. "Who said anything about being upset? I was just dancing for joy. Nice place, huh?"

"Why are the sheets on the furniture?" David asked.

"Mr. Whipple explains that in his notes," Joe said, looking at a sheet of paper. "He said he didn't know how long it would be before someone moved into the house, so he wanted to keep the furniture from getting too dusty."

"The sheets don't do much to help the floors," Wishbone said, noticing a dustball near his paws.

"Did Mr. Whipple mention what he did with Homer's personal belongings?" Wanda asked.

"He's written that Homer Hathaway's things are still here," Joe replied. "But when he has a chance, he'll help you clear away whatever you don't want. And he tells us in his notes where to find everything we might need for our visit."

"It's coming back to me," Wanda said, thinking as she moved slowly into one of the rooms on the left. "Being in this house, I mean. My parents and I came here one summer when I was seven years old. I remember how much I liked the house. It seemed so old, and there were so many great hiding places to explore."

The others followed Wanda into the room. Everyone moved slowly and cautiously.

Wanda lifted the slats of a shutter, letting a bit more sunlight into the room. "All of a sudden, I'm remembering Homer Hathaway a little better. He took a real liking to me. As I recall, he had a mischievous sense of fun. His wife, who died many years ago, was nice, too. I remember she had rosy cheeks. It's funny how being in a place you haven't seen for so long can bring back memories. It's almost like they're tucked away behind the drapes."

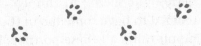

It seemed to Sam as if no one had lived in the house for centuries. And yet, at the same time, it felt as if people were living there now . . . even though the place had no one living there.

Sam felt goose bumps forming on her arms. She wasn't sure if they were because she was uneasy or because of the lack of heat in the house.

As Sam looked around the room, she gradually sensed that she was being watched. Then she realized why. Hanging on the walls were many oil-painting portraits. Each one showed the face of a person who had

lived a time long ago. Most of the men and women in the portraits wore dark clothing and stern expressions. Seen through the eerie light slicing in through the shutters, the portraits seemed to have some life in them.

"Who do you think all these portraits are of?" Sam asked Wanda.

"I imagine they're all different generations of Hathaways," Wanda said, looking closely at one of the paintings. "It's an age-old tradition for family members in New England to have their portraits painted and hang them in their homes."

The four humans and one dog wandered around the dusty room, but no one touched anything. It was almost as if everyone feared he or she might get scolded by one of the portraits.

Sam moved to a window. Through the partly closed shutter slats, she saw the gently moving blue water in the bay. She reached out to open the slats a bit more. Halfway there, her hand stopped.

Sam had become aware of a strange scratching noise.

"What was that?" Sam said quietly.

"You mean that scratching noise that sounded like a ghost?" Joe asked.

"Yes," Sam said, not sure if Joe was joking or not.

"It must be the wind," David said matter-of-factly.

"The wind *blows* or *sighs* or *wooshes*," Sam pointed out. "It doesn't *scratch*."

Again the scratching noise could be heard.

Sam felt her goose bumps growing larger.

David gave Joe a pat on the shoulder. "Joe, why don't you go check it out? You're the strongest. If there's something scary in here, you can take care of it."

"What good will my strength be against a ghost?" Joe said, playfully pushing David away.

"Oh, you guys are being silly," Wanda said, walking confidently across the room. "We'll all go check it out. It sounds like it's coming from this direction."

The group left the room and moved through the entrance hall. Then they entered a large kitchen.

At once, everyone broke into fits of laughter.

Wishbone had gotten up onto a kitchen counter. He was pawing at a cabinet, trying to get it open. His nails were the source of the scratching noise.

"I should have known," Joe said, lifting Wishbone down. "Whenever Wishbone visits a new house, he likes to investigate the food supply. Don't worry, big guy. I always make sure you get enough to eat, don't I?"

Wanda turned on the kitchen's overhead light.

Though the kitchen was far from modern, it looked much newer than the rest of the house. The floor was covered with linoleum, even though some holes let parts of the house's original wide floorboards peek through. Though the room was a bit out of date, at least there were appliances—refrigerator, gas stove, sink, washing machine, and dryer. Sam realized these things hadn't even been invented at the time the house had been built. A fireplace of rough-cut brick was set into a wall. Sam had never seen a fireplace before in a kitchen.

"Plenty of cleaning supplies," Wanda said after opening a closet door. "Now, let's take Wishbone's advice and see what the food supply is like."

David checked the refrigerator. "Nothing in the refrigerator but prunes and olives."

Joe checked the cabinets. "Nothing in the cabinets but flour, cooking oil, cereal, and tea."

Sam opened a door that led to a room-sized pantry. "Not much of any use in the pantry. Crackers, canned soups and sardines, and a few other odds and ends."

Wishbone was scouting around the floor for leftover crumbs.

"Here's what I think we ought to do," Wanda said. "The house is a bit cold, and I also think the place is making us all a little nervous. You kids bring our things in from the car. In the meantime, I'll try to figure out how to turn on the heat. Then we'll go into town for a while. We'll look around, get some lunch, and do some grocery shopping."

"Great idea," Sam said, closing the pantry door. "I feel like I could use some fresh air."

Chapter Three

Wishbone's black nose drew in the scent of salty sea air. The dog always found sea air refreshing. It also stirred up his appetite, but, then again, so did just about anything.

"Remember, guys," Wishbone called out, "our first order of business is lunch."

The dog trotted alongside Joe, Sam, David, and Wanda as they strolled along Front Street. They were in the center of Endicott's very small shopping area. The street was only a block away from the docks at the bay. Several times, the dog heard the screechy squawk of a seagull.

The town of Endicott seemed as if it sprang right out of an old novel set in a much earlier time period. Most of the stores and businesses were located in old-looking buildings. None of them was more than two stories high. Each structure had been built in the typical clapboard style. Each had been painted a different soft color—gray, white, cream, pale yellow, and light blue, among others.

Though the overall look of the town was old and weathered, everything seemed very clean and well maintained. Signs made of hand-painted wood hung in front of some of the shops. Halloween decorations were on display in a few of the windows. The public trash containers were made from old wooden barrels. Only a few local residents were walking along the street.

Wishbone saw a black cat slinking across the sidewalk just ahead of him and his friends.

Whenever Wishbone saw a cat, he felt a strong urge to chase after it. Even so, Wishbone was well aware that black cats were supposed to be bad luck.

Joe looked at Wishbone, as if sensing the dog's urge to chase the cat. "Let this one go, boy. We're just about to have lunch."

"Good point," Wishbone told Joe.

Soon the group stopped in front of a restaurant.

David read aloud the words on a striped awning. "'The Portside Tavern.'"

Sam read aloud a little sign on the door. "'No customers allowed without shirts, shoes, or compliments for the food. Dogs are welcome, though.'"

"This is great," Joe said with a smile. "We won't have to make Wishbone wait outside."

"Ha-ha! Very funny," Wishbone said. "Like there's really a chance I'd let you guys eat while I'm just standing outside watching the traffic. Er . . . maybe I should say the lack of traffic."

David opened the door and everyone entered. The Portside Tavern was a casual place with a seafaring look. Fishing nets were stretched across the ceiling, and beat-up boat lanterns hung from wooden posts. Wishbone's nose picked up the delicious aromas of freshly caught and cooked seafood. The restaurant wasn't too crowded, since it was just slightly past the regular lunch hour.

The group took seats at a table covered with a plastic red-and-white-checked tablecloth. Wishbone parked himself on the floor, right beside Joe's chair. The day's menu was hand-printed on a chalkboard that hung on one wall.

A sour-faced waitress came to the table. Without saying a word, she set down glasses of water, then waited for the orders. After everyone made their choice, the waitress walked away, still without saying a single word.

"She wasn't too friendly," Sam said.

Wishbone noticed two men at the next table eyeing his Oakdale group. They were rough-looking fellows, probably in their thirties. Both wore baseball caps and faded flannel shirts. They looked as if they could use a shave. Their plates were empty, but each man had a good grip on a mug of beer.

"Hi, there," Wanda said, giving the men a friendly wave.

One of the men gave a very slight nod.

"I'm thinking of taking ownership of a house here in Endicott," Wanda told the men. "I wonder if I might ask you gentlemen a few questions about the town."

The two men just stared.

"My name is Wanda Gilmore," Wanda said, seeming determined to strike up a conversation. "These are my friends—Joe, Sam, and David," she said, pointing to each one. "And that furry fellow hanging out down there is Wishbone. To whom do I have the pleasure of speaking?"

One of the men spoke in a gruff voice. "I'm Griffin. He's Scuffy."

Griffin was a muscular fellow. Scraggly blond hair and a single earring added an extra bit of toughness to his appearance.

Wishbone gave his side a scratch. *I know a dog named Duffy and a cat named Muffy, but Scuffy is a new one for me.*

"Scuffy," Wanda said pleasantly, "how did you get that name?"

"It's a long story," Scuffy mumbled.

And something makes me think he doesn't feel like telling it . . . like that scowl on his face.

Scuffy looked shorter than Griffin, but he seemed just as tough. He had a drooping moustache and a scar that sliced through his left eyebrow.

"Do the two of you live here?" Wanda asked.

"Yeah. Been here all our lives," Scuffy mumbled.

"We're lobster fishermen," Griffin said flatly.

Yeah . . . I thought that there was something fishy about these fellows.

"Is this your day off?" David asked.

After a swig of beer, Scuffy said, "Lobster fishermen don't get a day off. We're out on the water from sunup to sundown, seven days a week. No matter what the weather is. Some say it's the hardest work there is."

"The only reason we're not out on the water now is because our boat needs a complete overhaul," Griffin explained. "So we're just hanging out for a few days."

"Ah, well, that's nice," Wanda said, struggling to keep the conversation going. "I don't mean it's nice that your boat isn't working. It's just nice that you can enjoy having some free time. Uh . . . maybe you could tell me something. What's the weather like around here during the summer?"

"Kinda hot," Griffin grumbled.

"And the winter?"

After a belch, Griffin said, "Cold . . . wet."

Wishbone heard a whispered conversation among the kids.

"I don't think that these guys like us very much," Joe said.

"They sure seem suspicious of us for some reason," Sam agreed.

"I wonder why," David said.

"Why do you want to live around here?" Griffin said, squinting suspiciously at Wanda.

"Actually, I just inherited Hathaway House," Wanda explained. "I won't be living there on a year-round basis, but I think it might make a nice getaway home. It's so lovely around here, especially at this time of year."

Griffin and Scuffy looked at each other. Then they both broke into laughter.

Wanda wrinkled her brow. "What's so funny?"

After a swig of beer, Griffin said, "I wouldn't stay in Hathaway House if you gave me a million bucks."

"Not for two million," Scuffy added.

"Why?" Joe said. "Because you think the house might be haunted?"

Griffin pointed at Joe. "That's right, kid. You've hit the nail smack on the head. That house is haunted. And everyone around these parts knows it."

Scuffy gave a wheezing chuckle. "Ol' Homer Hathaway didn't mind too much, but then the old geezer was always a bit off his rocker."

"How do you know the house is haunted?" Sam asked with interest.

Griffin rose to his feet and dropped a few dollar bills on the table. "I was in there once at a New Year's party. I was wandering around in some of the rooms and I saw something so scary . . . well, it cut through me like a fierce nor'easter wind. Good day."

"And good luck," Scuffy said, getting up after draining the last drops of his beer.

"Uh . . . wait," Sam called out. "What did you . . ."

The two fishermen were already halfway out the door.

"Do you think they were just joking about the house?" Sam asked her friends.

"I couldn't tell," Joe said with a shrug.

"I'm sure they were joking," David said.

"I wonder if all lobster fishermen are that strange," Wishbone added. "Speaking of lobster, when's our food coming?"

Wishbone looked around the restaurant to see what

the other customers were eating. He suddenly noticed a shadowy shape perched on the outside of the front window. Wishbone took a better look and saw that it was a cat—the very same black cat that had crossed his path a few minutes earlier. The black cat seemed to be staring straight at Wishbone.

Its greenish-yellow eyes seemed to glow, as if they were powered by electricity.

That cat is almost daring me to go chase it, Wishbone thought. *Maybe I should. . . . No, maybe I shouldn't. Our food will be coming any minute now.*

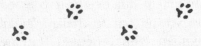

Sam noticed a beautiful black cat looking at them through the front window of the restaurant. She picked up her camera to photograph it. But by the time she aimed her lens, the cat had vanished.

"Hello, folks!" a voice boomed.

Sam turned to see a middle-aged man standing beside the table. He was a large man with wavy reddish hair. His shirtsleeves were rolled up, and an apron covered the front of his clothing. The lines around his eyes crinkled with friendliness. He reminded Sam of a young version of Santa Claus.

"Hello," Wanda said, speaking for the group.

"My name is Teddy Lyman," the man said. His deep voice seemed to echo as if it were coming from inside a cave. "I'm the owner of this humble eatery. How are you fine folks today?"

"We're just great," David answered.

Lyman gave a pleasant chuckle. "I hope those fishermen didn't bother you too much. Griffin and Scuffy aren't bad fellows, but they're not always so friendly. Especially not to out-of-towners."

Sam noticed that Lyman, like the fishermen, spoke with a regional accent. It was most noticeable with the *r*'s, which seemed to disappear. Instead of saying *aren't,* Lyman said *ahnt.*

"Oh, that's all right," Wanda said, smiling up at the heavyset man. "I always like meeting the local characters when I visit a new place. By the way, my name is Wanda Gilmore."

"I couldn't help but overhear your conversation," Lyman said, reaching out to shake Wanda's hand. "So you're the woman who inherited Hathaway House. I guess Oliver Whipple finally came to see you."

"That's right," Wanda replied. "Do you know Mr. Whipple?"

Lyman pulled an empty chair over to the table and lowered his big body into it. "Sure. I know everyone in this area. Whipple's a fine man, and a topnotch attorney. I knew Homer Hathaway, too. Terrible thing, him getting killed like that, way off in Greece. But he loved the sea, so I suppose it's fitting that he died at sea. Homer should feel right at home down there with all the fishes and algae and coral."

Sam shuddered at the thought. She liked the sea, too, but she couldn't imagine feeling at home on the bottom of it.

"I think it's wonderful that he was still sailing at his age," Wanda remarked.

"Yes, he was quite a guy," Lyman said. "If it hadn't been for that sailing accident, he probably would have made it to ninety or more. I imagine we'll hold some kind of memorial service for him in the next week or so."

"I met him only once, and it was a long while ago," Wanda said.

Lyman leaned in close to Wanda. "Well, I'm glad to meet *you*, Wanda Gilmore. I'm willing to make a deal with you. If, for some reason, you decide to sell Hathaway House, I'd appreciate being the first to know about it. You see, I've been wanting to open a bed-and-breakfast place in this town."

"What's a bed-and-breakfast?" Joe asked.

"It's like a little inn," Wanda told Joe. "But it's usually inside a regular house. The people who own the home rent out rooms, and a free breakfast comes with the price. It's cozier than staying in a hotel."

"They're very popular in New England," Lyman explained. "Especially in the warmer months. But we don't have one in this town yet. My sister is looking for a business to start, now that her kids are grown. This would be just the thing. She makes blueberry muffins that would make your mouth water. Anyway, I think Hathaway House would make a perfect bed-and-breakfast."

"Well, don't get your hopes up about taking over Hathaway House," Wanda warned. "I doubt I'll be selling it. I'd like to use it for myself and my friends as a getaway home."

"Have you stayed in the house yet?" Lyman asked.

"No. We just got here today," Wanda said. "But we'll be staying there for the next three nights."

"Do you think the house is haunted?" Sam asked.

A smile spread across Lyman's face. "Oh, it's kind of a local legend that Hathaway House is haunted. And, yes,

some people say they've seen strange things there. But I personally don't believe a word of it. All the same, the legend would be good for a bed-and-breakfast. Tourists eat that kind of thing up with a spoon."

"It adds to the atmosphere," Wanda said in a pretend-spooky voice.

Lyman grinned at Wanda. "That's absolutely right. Now, listen to me, Wanda Gilmore. Don't rush with your decision about the house. Stay there a few nights and see if you really like it. When are you planning to leave town?"

"Monday morning," Wanda said.

Lyman began to scribble some phone numbers on a napkin. "So why don't you get in touch with me before you leave? You can call me at these numbers, or you'll find me right here most days from about ten in the morning to nine in the evening. Let me know what you're thinking, one way or the other."

"I'll do that," Wanda said, taking the napkin and putting it in her purse.

Lyman stood up and swung his chair back to its regular position. "And, please, folks, let me know if there's anything Teddy Lyman can do to make your stay in town more pleasant. . . . Ah, here comes your food. Dig in!"

As Lyman left the table, the grumpy waitress set down the lunch orders in front of the diners. Everyone had chosen seafood. Joe and David both got platters piled high with fried clams, which looked a lot like crispy onion rings. Wanda got a bowl of steaming New England-style clam chowder, a creamy white soup filled with chunks of clams and potatoes.

Sam had ordered a lobster roll, which was something new for her. It looked simple but interesting. A soft white hot-dog roll was stuffed to overflowing with nice big chunks of lobster meat mixed together with mayonnaise and chopped celery.

The waitress left the table without saying a word.

Sam noticed Wishbone looking up at the table with great interest.

"We need to get an extra plate for Wishbone," Joe said, waving to get the waitress's attention.

As Sam examined the lobster roll in front of her, she realized that she was having mixed feelings about this trip. Sam had been drawn to Hathaway House by the rumors of it being haunted. However, she was finding the house and the town of Endicott a bit more spooky than she had bargained for.

Oh, come on, Sam told herself. *Despite what the fishermen said, the house probably isn't really haunted. There's nothing to be afraid of. There's no reason this trip shouldn't be a real treat. Just relax and have a terrific time.*

Sam lifted her lobster roll and took a bite. It was deliciously rich and creamy.

Chapter Four

Loaded with groceries, the group returned to the old, gray clapboard Hathaway House. After setting their bags on the kitchen table, everyone pitched in to put things away.

Somehow, the act of unpacking groceries made Sam feel more comfortable in the house. It also helped that the heat was on, giving the place a warmer temperature. Sam smiled as she watched Wishbone eye every food item go by him as if he were the referee at a sporting event.

When the last of the groceries were unpacked, Wanda said, "Now, what do you say we take a tour of the house? Let's see what, exactly, your friend Wanda has inherited."

Immediately, David made an interesting discovery. The kitchen's walk-in pantry had a door that led to another walk-in pantry. Built into a wall in the second pantry was a small door. When the door was raised, trays of food could be passed through the opening into the dining room.

"Oh, I get it," Wanda said, looking through the opening. "You see, the cook would come in here from the kitchen and could pass things to the butler in the dining room."

"Cook, butler," Sam said, impressed. "I guess Josiah Hathaway had quite a lot of money."

"Yes," Wanda said, brushing a spider web off a wall. "I believe the shipping business was very successful in those days. That was the time when the huge clipper ships were the main method of sea transportation all over the world."

Everyone went back through the kitchen and passed through a doorway that led to the dining room. Wanda and the kids went around the room, removing the white sheets from the furniture and folding back the shutters to let light in. They discovered that the shutters could slide into wooden compartments that were on the sides of the windows. Every window was framed by drapes, tied back with a sash.

Sam found the room much more cheery once it was filled with daylight. A long dining table was surrounded by high-backed chairs with stiff wicker seats and no cushions. A candelabra, a decorative holder containing eight upright candles, stood at the center of the table. Against one wall was a high glass-front cabinet filled with china plates and cups. Built into another wall was a fireplace that was made of rough-cut bricks. Beside it in a metal container lay a stack of cut-up logs.

"There seems to be a fireplace in every room," David noted. "That's kind of cool. Or maybe I should say 'hot.'"

Wanda knelt down to examine the fireplace. "That's because today's heating units didn't exist when the house

46

was built. The fireplace in the kitchen would have been used to give heat, and maybe for some of the cooking."

Sam waved a hand in front of her face. The sunlight had revealed hundreds of dust particles drifting through the air.

The group walked across the entrance hall. They went into the large room they had been in earlier in the day. Again, they removed the sheets and folded back the shutters. Most of the furniture was arranged around yet another brick fireplace. This room had plenty of places to sit—a wooden rocker, high-backed chairs, leather-upholstered armchairs, and a big Victorian sofa. Candles of different sizes stood in holders all around the room.

"This must be the living room," David said, feeling the fabric of a drape.

"Except they would have called it the 'parlor,'" Wanda said, folding a sheet.

Most of the furniture in the parlor and dining room was made from high-quality, well-crafted wood and seemed to be quite old. Except for the kitchen, all the floors were covered by darkly stained wide boards. Scattered all around on the floors were Oriental rugs of different sizes. Each rug was decorated with fascinating geometric patterns.

Most of the walls had wood paneling halfway up, with faded wallpaper covering the rest of the way. In addition to the many portraits on the walls, there were also some paintings of seascapes.

"I like the way the house is decorated," Sam said, examining the room with her artistic eye. "Everything is very nice, but not overly fancy."

Wanda was testing out the rocker. "The old-

fashioned New Englanders believed it was sinful to be too luxurious. Usefulness was more important to them than beauty. But they liked everything well made and built to last. I like it, too. Simple but homey."

"Hey, stop that," Joe told Wishbone.

The terrier was digging energetically at one of the Oriental rugs.

"It's bad enough that Wishbone digs in my flower garden," Wanda commented. "Now he's got to dig at my beautiful antique rugs."

"He won't do it anymore," Joe assured Wanda.

The group moved on and passed through a doorway that led from the parlor to a study. Once more, they removed sheets and opened shutters. Two adjoining walls of the study were filled, floor to ceiling, with books. There was an interesting desk, with an upper portion that could be hidden by a sliding panel of curved wood. Standing on the floor was a large globe of the world, its surface a tarnished gold color.

Wanda took a seat at the desk and ran a hand across the varnished wood. "Back in the 1800s, a gentleman always had a study. I can almost picture Josiah Hathaway sitting here, going over the books in which he recorded his shipping accounts. And, by the way, the women of the house usually weren't allowed into the study."

Sam examined a portrait that hung over the desk. It showed a middle-aged man wearing an old-fashioned black coat and a type of scarf around his neck. He was holding a map in his hands. His eyes, blue as the nearby bay, glinted with a cold expression. Just the hint of a smile rested on the man's lips. A plaque on the picture's frame said that the man was Josiah Hathaway.

"Pssst!" Sam whispered to the group. "This is Josiah Hathaway himself."

"Sir, I realize you don't approve of women in your study," Wanda told the portrait. "But I'm afraid your house now belongs to me."

The group returned to the entrance hall, where a tall grandfather clock stood guard. The face of the clock showed a painted sun shining down on a painted sailboat. The staircase leading up from the hallway consisted of a polished railing and bare wooden steps.

As the group climbed the staircase, Sam noticed that a few of the steps were warped and they creaked beneath her feet.

On the second floor, everyone walked down a hallway, then entered a large bedroom. Once they folded back the shutters, a three-sided window gave them a magnificent view of the bay. The room had the most beautiful bed Sam had ever seen. At each corner was a high wooden post that supported a canopy of green fabric trimmed with tassels. There were two solid dressers and a beautiful makeup table with a mirror. The glass of the old mirror was duller than a modern one, and it was speckled with rusty spots.

How many people have looked into this mirror through the years? Sam thought, as she leaned down to gaze at her reflection.

"This must be the master bedroom," Wanda said playfully. "I wonder which one of us should get to sleep in it."

All three kids pointed at Wanda.

"I was hoping you would say that," Wanda said with a wink. "After all, I am the owner of the house now."

The group continued the house tour and found three other bedrooms on the second floor. They were similar to the master bedroom, though not quite as large or nicely furnished. David picked one for himself because it contained a glass device that he recognized as a "Galileo thermometer." Joe picked another bedroom because it had a television.

Sam was holding out for something on the top floor.

The second floor also had a large bathroom. The bathtub, sink, and toilet looked usable, but not at all modern.

Wanda went into the room and turned on a faucet, testing the water flow. "This must have been converted from just a regular room into a bathroom. When the house was built, indoor bathrooms didn't even exist."

"Thank goodness for modern technology," David commented. "Personally, I like indoor facilities."

The group continued up the creaky staircase to the third, and top, floor. It was much less spacious than the lower two floors because it was actually right underneath the slanting roof. This floor had three small bedrooms and one small bathroom.

Moving down the hallway, Wanda said, "This floor would have been where the servants lived. And, if times turned hard, the family could rent out the rooms."

The group stepped into one of the bedrooms. The narrow bed was covered by a handmade quilt, which was decorated with colored patches of fabric. An antique music box sat on a small side table.

Halfway up from the floor, one wall slanted inward, following the angle of the roof. A small window jutted out from the slanted wall, overlooking the bay. Sam realized the window was part of the architectural feature Wanda had called a "gable."

Near the window hung a grouping of different-sized hollow metal tubes. Sam realized these were wind chimes. She gave the chimes a gentle push. The tubes brushed against one another, creating a pleasing, clinking noise.

"I think I'll take this room," Sam said. "It feels like the perfect hideaway."

"I guess that completes our tour," David said, as he led the others back into the hallway.

When they had walked downstairs to the first-floor entrance hall, Joe said, "So, Miss Gilmore, how do you like your new house?"

"I think I love it," Wanda said, knocking on the staircase's wooden railing. "It's comfortable and wonderful, and it's got some great secret nooks and crannies. On top of that, there is so much history inside these walls."

Sam picked a cobweb off the grandfather clock. *True, there's lot of history here. Maybe, just maybe, here there's a ghost or two mixed in with all the history.*

"So what's next?" Joe said, rubbing his hands together with eagerness. "How about a game of catch? I brought my football."

Wishbone's ears perked up at the idea.

"Not yet," Wanda said, assuming a businesslike manner. "First, there's work to be done. We need to make this place livable. I'll clean the kitchen and prepare dinner. Sam, go find all the towels and sheets. Then you can do the laundry. I hope the machine works. Joe, you can dust and vacuum the whole house. David, since you're so happy to have indoor bathrooms, you can clean them."

"Lucky me," David said humorously.

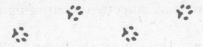

Wishbone made it his job to supervise the cleaning process.

He lay comfortably on a wooden shelf that stuck out from a window. He and Joe were in one of the second-floor bedrooms. As the dog enjoyed a patch of sunlight, he watched Joe move around the room, busily cleaning. Joe ran a feather duster across a dresser, sending flurries of dust flying through the air.

"Don't forget the corners," Wishbone reminded Joe.

After cleaning a few more spots, Joe began to dust the shutters attached to Wishbone's window.

Wishbone got up, grudgingly. *Oh, all right. I see I'll have to relocate.*

Wishbone jumped off the window shelf. He took a quick look around, then figured out a way to climb onto the old-fashioned high bed. He was pleased to find the bedspread was as soft as velvet. The dog dug at the bedspread with his paws, circled the spot a few times, then settled into a relaxing position.

Yeah, this feels really great. You know, all this cleaning is making me a bit sleepy. Maybe I should reward myself with a well-deserved nap.

Just as the dog's eyes began drooping, Sam burst into the room. She looked like a girl on a mission, hauling a laundry basket stuffed with sheets and towels.

Sam set down the basket and walked over to the bed. "Sorry, Wishbone, but I need to get to the sheets that are under you."

"Do you think you could come back later?" Wishbone

asked. "I must have forgotten to hang up the 'Do Not Disturb' sign."

"Off, boy," Sam said, as she began pulling back the bedspread.

Oh, this is ridiculous, Wishbone thought, leaping off the bed. *Maybe I'll go check on David.*

Wishbone ran down the hall. He found David in the large bathroom. The boy was kneeling by the bathtub, a bucket of cleaning supplies beside him. He turned one of the old-style faucet knobs, and a stream of slightly rusty water poured out.

The dog lay on the bathroom floor, enjoying the soothing coolness of the ceramic tiles. He watched David pour some powdery green stuff into the bathtub.

Wishbone's nose gave a strong twitch. *Yeccch! It smells like a chemical factory just blew up in here! This'll never do. Maybe I should go somewhere where the aromas are always pleasant.*

Wishbone raced down the hallway, trotted down the staircase, then made his way to the kitchen. Wanda was bustling around, in the middle of food preparation.

"What's for dinner?" Wishbone asked curiously.

Wanda was too busy to answer. She opened the refrigerator and pulled out a plate that was covered with clear wrapping, which she placed on the counter.

Oh, I'll just find out for myself.

Wishbone jumped onto a chair and, from there, it was just a short leap to the kitchen counter.

Wishbone glanced around at several plates and bowls of food items. *Aha! It looks as if we'll be having swordfish steaks, baked potatoes, and apple pie. Excellent!*

Wanda pulled a small glass bottle off a spice rack.

"Say, Wanda," Wishbone said in his nicest voice, "do you mind if I borrow one of these apple slices?"

When Wanda didn't reply, Wishbone figured it was all right. He lowered his muzzle toward a bowl of apples, all set to snatch a snack.

"Wishbone, down!" Wanda scolded.

Wishbone paused, wondering whether or not to take the apple anyway.

Better not push my luck, Wishbone thought, leaping off the counter. *Maybe I should go see how Joe is doing with his chores.*

As Wishbone hurried out of the kitchen, he was almost stepped on by Sam, who came charging in with her stuffed laundry basket.

Sam placed a big load of sheets into the washing machine and got them whirling away on the Hot cycle.

Having a little free time, Sam decided to explore. She wandered through the parlor, still feeling as if the portraits were staring at her. Then she went into the nearby study.

Sam spent some time looking at the many books that lined the shelves along the walls. The volumes were arranged, more or less, according to category—fiction, history, biography, ships, and many other topics. There were even a few books on the supernatural. Some of them were recent, but many looked like real antiques.

Sam's eyes were drawn to one of the older books. Bronze-tinted letters said: "*The House of the Seven Gables,* by Nathaniel Hawthorne."

Though Sam had heard of the book, she didn't know

anything about it. She hadn't even known what a gable was until that day. Interested, Sam pulled the book off the shelf. The binding was chocolate-brown, with flecks of maroon and gold running through it. The cover was beautiful, almost a work of art. Sam opened the book. The title page showed that the book had been printed in 1851.

Sam leafed through the book. The pages were a bit stiff and brittle, making a crinkly sound with each turn.

I brought a book with me, Sam thought. *But I think I'll read this one instead. I can probably finish it before I leave Hathaway House. Besides, it's got "gables" in the title, and I'm staying in a room with a gable. Perfect match.*

Sam felt a very slight swish of wind on her back. She turned around and saw that the door to the study was slowly closing. With a click, the door latched into the wooden door frame.

Keep calm, Sam thought, goose bumps rising on her arms. *I bet it's one of the guys playing a trick on me.*

After setting down the book on a nearby table, Sam went to the door and opened it. There was no one around.

Sam crossed the empty parlor, went through the entrance hall, and entered the kitchen. "Miss Gilmore, you didn't just close the door to the study, did you?"

"Not me," Wanda said, as she turned the oven on. "I've been right here preparing dinner."

Sam returned to the entrance hall and she called upstairs, "Joe! David!"

The vacuum cleaner shut off. Then Joe came over to the second-floor landing. "What is it, Sam?"

"Did you or David just close the door to the study?" Sam asked, somewhat suspiciously.

"No," Joe replied. "I've been cleaning one of the bedrooms, and David is cleaning the bathroom just down the hall."

Sam heard a toilet flush upstairs.

"Where's Wishbone?" Sam asked.

"In the bedroom with me," Joe said.

"While I was in the study, it seemed like someone closed the door. Are you sure one of you isn't trying to scare me?"

"No, we're not. Honest."

"Okay. Thanks."

Sam went back to the study and checked the door, swinging it back and forth a few times. The door seemed perfectly normal.

Well . . . doors close by themselves sometimes, Sam thought, picking up *The House of the Seven Gables. That's not so unusual. There must have been a draft. Sure, that must be what it was. . . . Right?*

Chapter Five

S am sat on the parlor sofa, her legs tucked underneath her. Whispering, she spoke to her friends.

"And then the door opened, ever so slowly. And who do you suppose was standing on the other side? A man with a scraggly beard and a scarred face and a patch over one eye. He was halfway between a man and a monster. And in his hand, he gripped a long, straight, glistening . . . razor."

Sam paused, pointing at Joe. The kids and Wanda were playing the game in which everyone took turns making up part of a story.

Joe took his turn. "In a trembling voice, the girl asked the man what he planned to do with the razor. Gruffly, the man replied, 'What do you think I'm going to do with it? Can't you see I need a shave?' The End."

Everyone laughed at the story's surprise comical ending.

Sam was having a great time. The dust and cobwebs had been cleared away a few hours ago, and the house was beginning to feel like a clean, comfortable, user-friendly home. A nice fire was crackling in the fireplace, warming Sam inside and out.

The others seemed to be enjoying themselves, too. David sat in an armchair, his feet propped on a footrest. Wanda rocked back and forth in her the rocking chair. Joe and Wishbone both lay on an Oriental rug near the fireplace.

The grandfather clock in the entrance hall sounded eight gongs, signaling that it was eight o'clock. Not long ago, everyone had eaten a delicious home-cooked dinner in the dining room. Afterward, all the diners, except Wishbone, pitched in to clear the table and wash the dishes. Now the only thing on the night's schedule was relaxation.

Joe got up and walked across the floor and opened an old wooden cabinet. Inside lay a somewhat out-of-date television and stereo system.

"Look—civilization!" Joe cried happily.

"Except that equipment looks older than me," David remarked. "Should we see how well the TV works?"

"Oh, let's not watch TV," Wanda suggested. "It's such a treat just to sit by the fireside in the company of good friends. Why don't we just have a nice, interesting conversation, instead?"

Joe returned to his place by Wishbone. "Okay. What should we talk about?"

After some thought, Wanda said, "Well, the three of you just started high school two months ago. How do you like it so far?"

"It's okay, I guess," Joe said with a shrug.

"Anything else?" Wanda urged.

"Well, the homework is a lot harder," Joe said.

"And the atmosphere seems more competitive," David added.

Sam twirled a lock of her blond hair. "When I walk through the halls at high school, everyone seems so . . . grown up. Some of the guys are six feet tall, and some of the girls look like models. And suddenly there's all this new pressure about grades and the social scene and . . . oh, I don't know. It just seems like everything is getting so complicated from only a year ago."

"And where do things go from here?" David said, looking a bit unsure. "After high school, it's straight to college. After that, right on to graduate school or a career."

"And somewhere in there," Joe said with a groan, "we might get married and have kids."

"Then it's just a few steps away from retirement," Sam said sadly.

Acting like a traffic cop, Wanda raised her hands. "Whoa, whoa, whoa! Everyone, please relax! Things don't happen quite that quickly. Look at me. I've been around for quite a while, and I'm still not at the retirement stage."

Sam smiled. Even though Wanda was in her early forties, she acted much younger than her age. She had plenty of adult responsibilities, such as owning and supervising her hometown newspaper, *The Oakdale Chronicle*. However, she was never stuffy or boring, and she got excited by things just the way a teenager did.

Wanda was single, but she spent so much time with Sam, Joe, and David that she was almost like a second mother to them. This was especially important to Sam, because Sam rarely saw her own mother. Sam's parents had divorced a few years back. It had been agreed that Sam would live with her dad, because her mother was frequently away on business trips.

"You're definitely not ready for retirement," Sam assured Wanda.

"Still, I know what all of you mean," Wanda said. "Getting older can be a bit scary."

Everyone fell silent. As Sam watched the flames jump around the logs, she grew fascinated by their mix of blue, yellow, and orange colors.

Sam turned her head. She saw that the door to the study was opening—slowly, silently, as if being pushed by unseen hands. After opening all the way, the door stopped moving.

Sam felt a chill run up her spine.

"Did anyone just see that?" Sam asked her friends.

"See what?" David asked.

"The door to the study just opened all by itself," Sam said with disbelief.

The others all looked at the opened study door. Even Wishbone turned his head in that direction.

"I thought it was already open," Wanda said.

"It was," Joe replied. "I was the last one in there, when I was dusting and vacuuming. And I'm positive I left the door open.

"Then at some point," Sam insisted, "it must have closed by itself. Because I'm sure I saw it open just a few seconds ago. And while we're on the subject, that same door closed by itself while I was in the study late this afternoon."

The others looked at Sam strangely, as if they didn't quite believe her.

"Well, don't worry about it," Wanda said with a casual movement of her hand. "Things like that happen in these old houses. It could be a draft, or it could be the house settling on its foundation."

Another silence fell over the conversation. Sam watched the ever-changing shapes of the fire. She imagined the flames were doing a dance, jumping around in a blaze of fiery color.

Could there really be a ghost somewhere in this house? Sam wondered.

Ever since Mr. Whipple had mentioned that Hathaway House was rumored to be haunted, Sam had been unable to stop thinking about ghosts. In fact, that was actually part of the reason Sam had been so eager to visit the house. At the same time, the idea of spirits worried Sam. Her thoughts on the subject seemed to go back and forth between fear and excitement, like a person riding a seesaw.

Sam was puzzled by her interest in ghosts. Though she liked a good ghost story, she had never been thrilled by them. When Sam and her friends rented a movie, the others often suggested one with a supernatural theme. Sam was more interested in movies that showed beautiful visuals.

As far back as Sam could remember, she had been drawn to art. Over the years, she went from coloring books to finger painting to sketching to watercolors. Finally, Sam had been introduced to photography, which had become her main hobby. Sam's dad had recently bought her a very sophisticated camera. She carried it around with her much of the time.

Sam wasn't sure why she was so attracted to photography. Perhaps it was the way a photograph could capture a passing moment and freeze it just the way it was.

Still staring at the fire, Sam said, "Do any of you believe in ghosts?"

"Nope," David said with certainty.

"As you all know, I used to believe in them," Joe said, petting Wishbone's back. "But now . . . no, I don't believe in them."

"I go back and forth on this subject," Wanda said, rocking in her chair. "Right now, I tend to doubt that ghosts exist. But I like to keep an open mind about the idea. What about you, Sam?"

"Before I got here," Sam said, trying to form her thoughts, "I didn't really believe in ghosts. But this house seems so . . . haunted. I'll put it this way. Under the ghost file in my mind, there's a big question mark."

"Sam, look," David said, going into his technical tone. "It's just not scientifically possible. The human body is made up of muscles, flesh, nerves, tissue, blood, and a few other things. When a person dies, those things no longer work. They're through. Gone for good. End of story."

"Isn't there some scientific theory that says energy can't be created or destroyed?" Wanda mentioned.

"That's right," Sam agreed. "When a person dies, maybe his or her energy just moves into a different type of form—you know, like the way wood changes into fire."

"That's partly true," David admitted. "But a dead person's body mixes with the ground, and then it helps the earth produce other life forms. But that doesn't mean a person's physical energy can start roaming through a house, walking through walls or whatever. Come on, it's almost the twenty-first century. It's time for modern science to replace old-world superstition."

"In the fifteenth century," Sam argued, "even the scientists and great thinkers wouldn't have believed anything like television or computers would be possible. There *must* be things we don't know about yet."

"There are," David said, growing a bit frustrated. "But ghosts aren't one of them!"

"You have to admit that many people claim they've seen ghosts," Wanda pointed out. "And not all of these people are unreliable. I bet each of us knows at least one person who thinks he or she has seen evidence of a ghost."

Joe scratched Wishbone's head. "Maybe some people like to believe in ghosts because they like to think life continues forever."

That could be true, Sam thought, staring at the fire.

"My feelings on the subject are a lot like Sam's," Wishbone told his friends. "On the one paw, I realize that ghosts aren't really possible. But, on the other paw, the thought of ghosts scares the heck out of me. So what does that mean? Well, to be honest, I don't know. And, for the record, I think I saw that door opening, too."

No one seemed to hear any of Wishbone's words of wisdom.

Wishbone spoke to the fire, even though he knew it couldn't hear him. *I say the most amazing things, but sometimes people just don't listen. Why is that?*

Wishbone shifted into a different position. He was

really starting to enjoy the Oriental rug near the fireplace. The worn-down wool material had the perfect mix of softness and scratchiness. Wishbone also liked the rug's colorful, almost magical, patterns. He liked to think that it was a flying carpet imported from some ancient land in the mysterious Far East.

Suddenly, Wishbone's tail bristled.

Like many dogs, Wishbone had a sixth sense that often told him things—like the next day's weather; if food was about to be served; when a nearby person or animal was afraid. At the moment, the sense was telling him that he was being watched.

Wishbone glanced around the room at the different portraits. Every single picture seemed to be watching the dog. But Wishbone felt his tail had been reacting to something . . . more alive.

The dog's eyes roamed to one of the parlor windows. He got up and moved to the window. It was an old-style

window in which many small panes of glass were separated by strips of wood. It was completely dark outside. But Wishbone did see something out there—a pair of greenish-yellow eyes.

Wishbone's tail jumped. *It's the black cat! The same one I saw earlier today. Twice.*

Wishbone could make out the cat's shadow-black body against the night. The creature was perched on the outside windowsill. It was staring inside, straight at Wishbone and his friends.

I'm keeping my eye on you, buster. But then, it seems you're also keeping your eyes on me.

Wishbone and the black cat stared at each other, as if daring the other to look away first.

Maybe I should go out there and show that cat how dogs can be bad luck for black cats. . . . No, I don't think I will. He moved away from the window and went back to the rug. *I'm so comfortable here on this rug. Why are black cats considered bad luck, anyway? There must be a good reason for it. Or maybe not. Maybe somebody just made up that superstition for the fun of it.*

The cat's eyes seemed as if they might burn a hole through the window pane.

Wishbone glanced around the parlor at his friends, who were still talking to one another.

I sense there's danger about. My friends are going to need a reliable watchdog. Tonight, while the others sleep, I'll stay awake.

Chapter Six

Sam lay tucked snugly under the patchwork quilt of her bed in her small bedroom on the top floor of Hathaway House. She rested her back against two pillows that she had propped against the headboard.

It was a little past ten o'clock, and everyone had gone to bed for the night. Though Sam and her friends had gotten up very early that morning, Sam wasn't quite ready for sleep. By the light of a lamp on a nightstand next to her bed, she had just begun to read *The House of the Seven Gables*.

The first few pages described the house itself. They began: "Half-way down a by-street of one of our New England towns, stands a rusty wooden house, with seven acutely peaked gables facing toward various points of the compass, and a huge, clustered chimney in the midst."

The book had been published in 1851. As in many books written a long time ago, the writing style was somewhat difficult. The long sentences twisted and turned, reminding Sam of the complex patterns that decorated Hathaway House's Oriental rugs. But, in a way, the old-time writing style made it much easier for Sam to let her imagination wander into a faraway time and place.

Sam turned a stiffened page of the old book.

The first chapter was set in the late 1600s. A rich and respected man, Colonel Pyncheon, just had the handsome House of the Seven Gables built for himself. He picked the land for the house because running underneath it was a fresh-water spring, which could be drawn up from a well.

The land had previously contained a simple cottage built by a poor man named Matthew Maule. For years, Colonel Pyncheon had tried to get the land away from Maule by using legal methods. When that failed, Pyncheon had Maule arrested for practicing witchcraft. The people of New England in those days believed in witchcraft, and they considered it a very serious crime.

After a court trial, Matthew Maule was sentenced to death. As Maule stood on the gallows, about to be hanged, he pointed an accusing finger at Colonel Pyncheon. The condemned man said, "God will give him blood to drink."

After Matthew Maule's death, the colonel easily took possession of the poor man's land. On the day the colonel moved into the House of the Seven Gables, he invited the local leaders of the town to a house-warming party. Upon arriving, the guests discovered the colonel sitting in a chair, holding a pen, staring at them curiously. Though his eyes were open, the man was dead. His beard and shirt collar were stained with blood.

The cause of the colonel's death remained a mystery. However, many people in town believed that he had choked on his own blood—as a direct result of Matthew Maule's awful curse.

Sam paused in her reading. She had become aware of a gurgling sound. Sam immediately thought of Colonel Pyncheon. Amazingly, the gurgling sounded very much like someone choking on their own blood.

I know it's possible to really get into a book, Sam thought, *but this is ridiculous. I seriously doubt that sound could be what I think it is. But what is it?*

Sam felt she had to investigate. Maybe one of her friends was injured. If so, they would need her help. And if the sound turned out to be nothing important, she would discover that, too. Otherwise, she would stay up all night worrying.

She climbed out of bed and left the room, wearing her flannel pajamas. Sam crept along the hallway. Then, gripping the railing, she made her way down the dark staircase. Sam's weight made the steps creak as she walked.

As Sam reached the second floor, the gurgling sound stopped briefly. Then it started again.

It's definitely coming from the second floor.

The hallway was lit only by a thin shaft of light, which came from the almost closed bathroom door. Sam crept quietly toward the bathroom. With every step, the gurgling grew louder.

Sam knocked softly at the door. It opened.

Sam gasped when she saw a ghostly white face.

A second later, Sam realized it was only Wanda in a bathrobe, her face smeared all over with cream. Then Wanda tilted her head back, continuing her activity. She was gargling.

After spitting some liquid in the sink, Wanda said, "Hi, Sam. What brings you down here at this time of night?"

Sam couldn't help but laugh with a sense of relief. "I was reading about a death scene in *The House of the Seven Gables,* and I thought that you might be choking on your own blood."

"I'm happy to say I'm not choking," Wanda said, looking confused. "My throat was starting to feel a little sore. So I gargled with some warm saltwater. Best thing for a sore throat."

"I'm just glad everything's okay." Sam smiled.

Sam made her way back upstairs to her room. She slipped back under the covers. Then she let her mind slip back into the *The House of the Seven Gables*. After another dozen pages, Sam had finished the first chapter. Feeling wide awake, she kept reading.

A short while past midnight, Sam set the book on her nightstand and turned off the lamp.

Time drifted by. . . .

Sam eased her eyes open, feeling as if she were floating through the air on a fluffy cloud. She had no idea if she had been asleep for a few hours or just a few minutes.

She became aware of a nearby noise. It was eerie, yet pleasing.

Sam rolled onto her other side. Peering across the dark room, she saw the window, which was set into the roof's gable. As her eyes adjusted to the darkness, Sam made out the tubelike shapes of the wind chimes.

The wind chimes were moving, ever so slightly.

As the hollow metal tubes clinked against one another, they created a chorus of light, jangling tones.

That's odd, Sam thought, sitting up slowly. *I can plainly see that the window is shut. Where is the breeze coming from? There must a breeze, or else the wind chimes wouldn't be moving.*

Sam lifted a hand, slowly moving it back and forth. There wasn't the faintest trace of a breeze, at least not by the bed.

Could it be . . . a ghost?

Sam felt a brief spark of nervousness.

Maybe the boys are trying to scare me. . . . No, they wouldn't pull a prank like this, not right in the middle of the night. . . . Oh, what's the big deal? There's probably a draft coming from that old window frame. The sound of the wind chimes is really very soothing. I'll just go right back to sleep.

The moment Sam's head touched the pillow, another

sound began to mix with that of the wind chimes. The new sound was similar, but different. It was music—tiny, high-pitched notes that sounded as if they were coming from a doll-sized piano.

Maybe Joe is watching TV in his room. Or maybe a clock radio went off somewhere. Or . . .

Sam remembered that there was an antique music box in her bedroom. But she knew that a music box could play only if it had been wound and if the lid was up. Sam didn't remember the lid being up, and she certainly hadn't wound the box herself.

But those notes sound exactly like what comes out of a music box. And they're coming from the exact direction of where I last saw the music box. It must be . . .

Sam forced herself to sit up again. Through the darkness she could make out the shape of the music box on the table. The lid seemed to be up.

Okay, now I'm spooked! Someone—or something—made that music box play just now! And since I don't see anyone, it must be a—

"Hello?" Sam said in a raspy whisper. "Is anyone here?"

Sam heard nothing but the pleasing notes of the music box. By then, the wind chimes had settled into silence.

Sam's breath seemed to stop. She thought about crossing the room to examine the music box. But she realized she preferred not to leave the safety of her bed.

This isn't happening, this isn't happening, this isn't . . .

Suddenly, the music box stopped playing.

Sam stayed motionless—waiting, watching, listening. All was silent.

Should I call for the others to come? Yes, I . . . No, I'd better not. That'll just get everyone all upset, and maybe over nothing. There must be a totally logical explanation for what just happened here. Unfortunately, I don't have the slightest idea what it might be.

Sam ran a hand up and down one arm, checking to make sure she wasn't locked inside a dream. It didn't seem that she was. Still, she discovered that the act of rubbing her arm was helping her to feel somewhat calmer. She continued rubbing her arm for a few minutes.

Why don't I just try to sleep? Sam thought finally. *Maybe the answers will sort themselves out with the morning sun. They usually do.*

Sam lay her head on the pillow, closing her eyes.

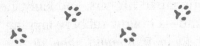

Wishbone opened his drowsy eyes.

Huh? . . . What? . . . Wishbone thought groggily. *Have I been . . . sleeping? Uh-oh, I was supposed to stay awake all night, watching for signs of danger. Ah, well, it happens to the best of us watchdogs.*

The dog lifted his head a bit. He was lying at the foot of Joe's bed in one of the second-floor bedrooms. Joe was fast asleep under the covers. The room was a shadowy world of darkness.

Something made me wake up. What was it? The last thing I remember, Wanda was gargling, and Sam came down to talk to her. Pretty soon after that, I got tired and then shut my eyes for a . . .

Wishbone poked his black nose into the air. In addition to smelling the room's usual scents, he was picking up something different. The aroma was a cross between the sharpness of medicine and the sweetness of perfume.

Hmm . . . that scent is familiar to me. It's a type of cologne some men splash on their face. The guy at the grocery store in Oakdale always wears it. What's it called? . . . It's . . . it's . . . Bay Rum! That must have been what woke me up. But where could it be coming from? I know for sure that neither Joe, Sam, David, nor Wanda wears Bay Rum.

Wishbone sat up, gave himself a good paw scratch, then looked around the room. He saw only the darkened outlines of the furniture, drapes, and the old-style TV set with the long antennae. The sounds were all normal, too—Joe's slow breathing, the steady ticks of the clocks in the house, the distant sound of the ocean waves breaking.

Wishbone raised his ears. Suddenly, he was picking up a new sound—a hollow-rubbery-tapping.

Bummff. Bummff. Bummff. Bummff.

Wait a second! I know that sound. It's a ball bouncing! One of my favorite noises! Who could be doing that? Neither

Sam, David, nor Wanda would be bouncing a ball in the middle of the night. Joe might, but he's right here, sleeping in the bed.

After a few moments, the sound of the bouncing stopped.

Wishbone turned his eyes to the windows. They revealed nothing but the night's blackness.

This is so strange. Maybe that wasn't really a ball bouncing. Maybe it was just the heating pipes or something else mechanical. And maybe the Bay Rum was . . . well, maybe it was just the smell of the nearby bay. Sure, those could be the right explanations. Unless . . . well, I don't want to think about that right now.

Wishbone shifted into a new position, keeping his eyes watchful.

Everyone is going to be just fine. Nothing to worry about. The world's finest watchdog is on the job.

Soon, however, the dog's eyelids began to droop.

Chapter Seven

SATURDAY

"Good morning!" Wanda said brightly.

Sam had just strolled down the two flights of stairs and entered the kitchen. Though she had already washed, brushed her teeth, and dressed, she still felt a lingering drowsiness.

Joe, David, and Wanda were seated at the kitchen table, each looking fresh and alert. Wishbone bent over a bowl, finishing the last nibbles of his breakfast. It was a cloudy morning, but soft beams of sunlight managed to filter through the kitchen windows.

"'Morning, everyone," Sam said, as she took a seat at the table.

"You slept late," Joe said, as he poured Sam a glass of orange juice. "It's ten past nine. Miss Gilmore already went for a power walk, and David, Wishbone, and I played some catch outside."

David got up and brought a plate of corn muffins to the table. Joe went to get some butter and jam out of the refrigerator.

"I stayed up late reading *The House of the Seven Gables,*" Sam said after taking a sip of juice.

Sam didn't mention the wind chimes or the music box. Soon after waking up that day, she had remembered the strange happenings during the night. She had even examined the music box and found it to be perfectly normal—it worked only if Sam wound a knob and then opened the lid. But, in the fresh light of morning, the strange happenings seemed like the leftover memories of a dream. Sam figured she would mention these things when she felt the time was right.

"Tell us about it," Wanda urged.

At first Sam thought Wanda was talking about the music box and wind chimes. Then she realized Wanda was talking about *The House of the Seven Gables.*

As Sam spread raspberry jam on a muffin, she told everyone about the events of the book's first chapter. Colonel Pyncheon had arranged for Matthew Maule to be hanged for practicing witchcraft. Then she told them about Maule's curse: "God will give him blood to drink." Sam explained how the colonel had built the House of the Seven Gables on Maule's land, and that the colonel had died on his first day in the house.

As they ate their muffins, Joe, David, and Wanda seemed to hang on Sam's every word. Sensing their interest, Sam moved into the next part of the story.

"The second chapter skips from the late 1600s to the middle of the 1800s," Sam said, breaking off a piece of muffin. "The House of the Seven Gables still belongs to the Pyncheon family, but it's now lived in by Hepzibah Pyncheon. She's an elderly lady who's always scowling, even though she isn't really mean. She rents a room to someone named Holgrave. He's this nice gentleman. And he makes daguerreotypes for a living."

"He makes *what?*" Joe asked.

"Daguerreotypes were among the earliest kinds of photographs," Sam explained. "I saw one in a museum. They show an image that's similar to regular photographs, but they're dimmer, and they're on thin, square pieces of metal instead of on paper."

"Hmm . . . I never knew that," Joe said.

"Then Hepzibah's cousin, Phoebe, comes to live at the house," Sam continued. "She's young and pretty, and she has a really sunny personality. I get the feeling there may be some romance developing between her and Holgrave. Then, a little later, Hepzibah's brother, Clifford, comes to live in the house. He's an older man with long gray hair, but he acts really strange and childlike. You get the sense he's not quite right in the head. Clifford has been away from the house a long time, but I don't know why yet."

"So you have these four people living in the house," David said, in between bites of his muffin. "What keeps things interesting?"

"Not that much happens," Sam replied. "But the house is filled with this sense of . . . doom. You get the feeling the house may be haunted."

"By who?" David asked.

"By Matthew Maule and his curse about drinking blood," Sam answered.

After a sip of orange juice, Wanda said, "Speaking of which . . . I guess Hathaway House isn't haunted after all. Has anyone seen a sign of a ghost yet?"

Joe and David shook their heads.

Now that Sam was more awake, she felt more brave. She decided to describe her experience from the previous night.

"Uh . . . well . . . It seemed like something very strange happened in my room last night."

Everyone looked eagerly at Sam. Even Wishbone looked up at her with great interest. After she took a deep breath, Sam told the others about the wind chimes and the music box. When Sam was done, Wanda, Joe, and David looked at her with puzzlement.

"Sam, if you like," Wanda said very kindly, "you can stay with me in my room tonight."

"You must have been dreaming," Joe said, trying to be helpful.

David gave Sam a reassuring pat on her arm. "Or maybe you're just thinking about ghosts so much that you convinced yourself there must be one in the house."

I wonder if I might have been just dreaming, Sam thought, staring at the empty brick fireplace across the room. *But I can't remember ever having a dream that seemed so real.*

Sam noticed Wishbone staring up at her. His brown eyes seemed to burn with the desire to say something. Sam figured the dog was just eager to get a piece of her muffin.

"Listen up, everybody," Wishbone said excitedly. "Some weird stuff happened in my room, too. I tried to tell Joe about it earlier, but he just wouldn't listen. I smelled Bay Rum and I heard a ball bouncing!"

No one paid much attention to Wishbone's words.

"Joe, Sam, David, Wanda—listen to me!" Wishbone pleaded. "I didn't think too much about it at the time. But now that I know what happened to Sam, I think it must be something in the supernatural category! Any comments?"

Still no one responded.

Wishbone gave his side an irritated scratch. *They're taking my story even less seriously than they're taking Sam's story. But I know what I smelled, and I know what I heard. For barking out loud, who smells or hears better than a dog?*

Wanda seemed eager to move away from the ghost subject. "Sam, do you know anything about Nathaniel Hawthorne, the author of *The House of the Seven Gables*?"

"Last year we read one of his short stories in class," Sam said. "It was called 'Young Goodman Brown,' and it had some cool supernatural stuff in it. Our English teacher said Hawthorne was the first American author to be really respected as a writer throughout the world. And I know his most famous book is *The Scarlet Letter*, which some of the kids are reading in senior English."

"Well, he grew up not far from here, in Salem, Massachusetts," Wanda pointed out. "Most of his novels and short stories are set in the colonial New England region. And all of you know about the Salem witch trials, right?"

The three kids nodded.

Wishbone perked up his ears. He knew about the Salem witch trials, too.

Back in 1692, some girls had gathered on a few occasions to dance around without any clothes on in a forest near Salem, Massachusetts, pretending to be witches. When the leading citizens of Salem heard about this, they thought it was a sign that some kind of evil had fallen over the young people. Being deeply religious folks, the town leaders were especially afraid of witches or anything else of a devilish nature. Fear spread through the town like wildfire. Townsfolk were instructed to turn in to the authorities people who might be possessed. Within half a year, nineteen people—young and old, men and women—had been put on trial and hanged as witches, even though they were all really innocent.

It reminds me of the last time I was wrongfully locked up in the Oakdale dog pound. Oh, the unfairness!

Wanda leaned forward. "Well, one of the judges at the Salem witch trials was an ancestor of Nathaniel Hawthorne's. His name, I think, was Colonel John Hathorne. Nathaniel was so ashamed that one of his relatives had sentenced innocent people to die that he added a 'w' to his last name. He didn't want their names spelled the same way."

Sam nodded thoughtfully. "So the book's character of Colonel Pyncheon must have been based on Colonel Hathorne in real life. Interesting. I love hearing about the things that inspire authors to write stories."

As the group continued discussing Nathaniel Hawthorne, Wishbone began pacing the linoleum floor. An idea was brewing in his head.

Witches, witches, witches. That reminds me of the mysterious black cat I saw looking in the window last night. I think I heard once that black cats are somehow connected to witches. What was it I heard? Maybe . . . that black cats are really witches in feline form. That would be just like a cat, wouldn't it?

Wishbone stopped pacing.

Hey, if that's the case, the black cat might have something to do with the mysterious stuff that's been happening around here. Note to myself: I need to investigate the matter of this black cat further.

Wanda sprang up from her chair. "Now that I've done my educational duty, I think I'll have myself a cup of black coffee."

"Hey, Wanda," Wishbone called, "while you're up, how about frying a few slices of bacon for me? Thanks."

Wanda didn't get to the bacon right away. Instead, she filled a teakettle with water, placed it on the stove, then turned on the bluish gas flame. Wishbone grew hopeful when he saw Wanda doing something else at the counter. But, as it turned out, she was only getting a spoon, a mug, and a jar of instant coffee.

Wheeeeeeee!!

The shrill shriek of a whistle pierced Wishbone's sensitive ears.

Wanda stared at the kettle with disbelief.

"Is your water boiling already?" Joe called over the harsh whistling. "Didn't you just put it on?"

"Just . . . just . . . just this very m-moment," Wanda stammered.

"I *saw* you do it," David said, looking very puzzled.

Wanda turned off the flame, causing the whistling to fade. She picked up the teakettle and poured some water into the mug. Steam drifted up.

Joe went to the mug. "This is impossible. Water can't boil that fast." Joe stuck a finger in the mug, then quickly pulled it out. "Ouch! It's boiling, all right."

Everyone stared at the mug of steaming liquid, shocked.

"Miss Gilmore, don't use that water," David warned. "Something may be wrong with it."

Sam stood up. "I was right! Even though I can't explain it, I know something ghostly is in here with us. Maybe now all of you will believe me about the doors and the wind chimes and the music box!"

"And the bouncing ball!" Wishbone exclaimed. "Let's not forget about the bouncing ball!"

Wanda looked around the kitchen with helpless confusion. "Something weird *is* happening in Hathaway House!"

Chapter Eight

David went to the teakettle and pulled off the lid. He tried to look inside. Then he picked up a long spoon, which he stirred around inside the kettle. He saw nothing but watery darkness and steam.

"This was some kind of trick," David told the others. "If I had my chemistry equipment here, I could probably figure out how it was done."

"Unless . . ." Sam looked around at everyone in the group. "Unless a ghost caused that water to boil."

Wanda sank into a chair. "Maybe all the rumors are true. With what Sam has experienced, and now the kettle, maybe the house *is* haunted."

"Oh, I doubt it's really haunted," Joe said, glancing around the kitchen. "All the same . . ."

"This house is *not* haunted," David stated. "Sam, maybe you really did see and hear all those strange things, but that doesn't mean they were caused by a ghost. It's very important for us not to jump to conclusions."

David took a seat at the table. As far back as David

could remember, he had been fascinated by science. He could recall the day he asked his first-grade teacher about the mechanical workings of the school's intercom system.

David liked the way science could break down something that seemed mysterious and explain it in a logical way. With step-by-step scientific investigation, practically anything in the world could be analyzed and understood. All it took was a little patience and intelligence.

And, in the world of science, nothing was accepted as fact until it could be proven by hard evidence. David didn't like to believe in anything strange unless he could see it proven—without any doubt—before his own eyes.

David knew that he had worried about ghosts a few times when he was younger. But, to this day, David had never seen any proof that ghosts existed. Besides, from a purely scientific viewpoint, David knew the existence of ghosts was an impossibility.

"If the house *isn't* haunted," Wanda told David, "then what do you think is going on?"

"It's obvious—someone is playing a prank on us," David said calmly. "This person must be trying to make us *think* the house is haunted."

"That would be a pretty mean prank," Wanda said, frowning. "Who would do such a thing?"

Sam said, "If this is a prank, how about those two lobster fishermen we met yesterday? Griffin and Scuffy didn't seem to like us just because we were from out of town. I'd say they're prime suspects."

"And what about Mr. Lyman, the owner of the Portside Tavern?" Joe said. "He seemed really eager to buy the house from Miss Gilmore. Maybe he thinks he can force her to sell the place by making her believe it's haunted."

"We should pay a visit to Griffin and Scuffy," David suggested. "And we should also pay a visit to Mr. Lyman. Maybe we can get some idea whether or not one of them is behind the prank."

"The sooner the better," Wanda said, tapping the table nervously. "Let's do it this morning. I want to know what's going on around here."

"Here's another idea," Sam said. "Mr. Whipple mentioned that Homer Hathaway had a few other relatives. What if one of those relatives was angry that Miss Gilmore was the one getting the house? Maybe this relative is trying to scare her away, hoping that he or she will end up with the house."

David nodded. "That's not a bad theory."

"But I don't know who those relatives could be," Wanda said, still tapping the table. "They might even be on Homer's wife's side of the family."

"Here's what really bothers me," Joe said seriously. "If someone is pulling a prank on us, that means whoever it is must be getting inside the house without us knowing about it."

Wanda wrinkled her brow, trying to remember something. "I'm sure I locked all the doors last night. Maybe this person has a key. Maybe I should hire a locksmith to come change the locks?"

"That may not help," David said. "It's pretty obvious we're dealing with a very tricky person. If this person has the knowledge to make water boil almost instantly, this person can easily slip past a lock. What we need is some kind of security system. It may not keep someone out of the house, but at least it will let us know *if* someone is sneaking into the house."

David got up and began searching through several drawers in the kitchen. Soon he found what he needed—a roll of clear tape and four butter knives. He set the items on the table.

David raised a finger to his lips, indicating that the others shouldn't say anything. Then David checked out the kitchen, just to make sure no one was hiding there. He even did a search of the walk-in pantry. Wishbone snooped around the room alongside David. They didn't find anyone.

"We need to be quiet," David whispered, taking a seat at the table. "There's a slight chance someone could be hiding near the house. This tape will be our security system."

"How?" Joe asked in a whisper.

"It works like this," David whispered. "We cut the tape into little strips. We place a strip on the inside of every door and window in the house. The strips will be practically invisible. If someone tries to get inside a door or window at any time, the tape will be torn away. That'll tell us there's been an intruder. We'll keep the tape in place at all times, and we'll just keep checking it."

David tore off about sixty strips of tape, which he placed on the four different butter knives.

Wanda passed out the knives. "This is brilliant thinking, David. Sam, you tape the top floor. I'll tape the second floor. Joe and David can do the ground floor."

"Wait," David whispered. "There's more. While we're going around the house, we need to check every possible hiding place. We need to make sure no one is hiding here in the house right now. Leave no stone or bedspread unturned. Oh, and one more thing. Keep a

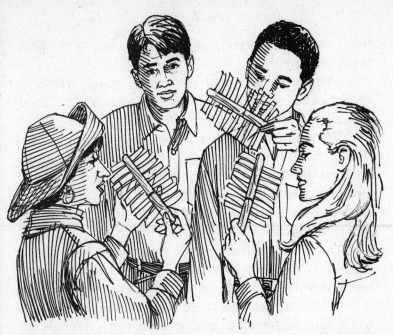

lookout for some kind of secret passageway that leads into the house. Sometimes you find them in these old homes. Okay, let's get to work."

Sam and Wanda took their knives with tape attached and headed upstairs. Joe and David, using their own knives, began taping up the doors and windows in the kitchen.

"I found a secret passageway," Wishbone whispered.

When Joe didn't seem to hear, Wishbone gave the boy's leg a nudge. Joe crouched down to see a swinging doggie door near the bottom of the kitchen door leading outside. Joe pulled David over.

"Nothing bigger than a dog or cat could get through

this," David whispered, checking the door. "I wouldn't worry about it."

That black cat could get through there, Wishbone thought with concern. *But if the cat is really a witch, it can probably just walk through the wall, too.*

Wishbone continued snooping and sniffing around the kitchen. The dog enjoyed sinking his teeth into a good mystery almost as much as he enjoyed chewing on a meaty bone. Besides, with his many special senses and talents, Wishbone considered himself to be one of the best canine detectives in the business.

Once the kitchen was all taped and checked, the boys and Wishbone moved on. Joe went to the dining room. David and Wishbone went to the entrance hall.

Wishbone realized there were hundreds of places where someone could be hiding or where a secret passageway could be located. Searching through Hathaway House was like digging through the soil of a stranger's backyard. The deeper he dug down, the less he knew what to expect.

David found a door in the side of the staircase. Inside that was a storage space for firewood. David crawled around in there, but found no sign of a passageway.

"I found another secret passageway in the hallway," Wishbone whispered.

When David didn't seem to hear, Wishbone pawed at the floor, right where the outline of a secret door lay.

David came over and saw part of a trapdoor in the floorboards. After moving a rug aside, he found a hand slot and managed to lift the trapdoor. He saw what seemed to be a basement, pitch-dark.

"Joe, come here," David called in a whisper. "And

bring two lit candles from the parlor. A flashlight would be better, but I don't know where one is."

Moments later, Joe came into the entrance hall with two lit candles. He and David climbed down a few steps leading into the basement. Wishbone quickly formed a rear guard.

"If there is a secret passageway," David whispered to Joe, "this would be the best place for it. Check everything very carefully."

The basement area was only about four feet high. Wishbone could move around easily, but Joe and David were forced to crouch down on their hands and knees. By the flickering candlelight, Wishbone could see that the walls were made of stone. There wasn't anything in the basement but cobwebs and a bone-chilling dampness.

Then . . . Wishbone saw a pair of eyes staring at him!

Before the dog had a chance to become too startled, he realized the eyes weren't real. They belonged to a piece of wood, carved and painted to look like a mermaid.

Joe crawled over, holding his candle near the mermaid's face. The flickering flame almost seemed to breathe life into the wooden figure.

"David, check this out," Joe whispered. "I think this is one of those things that were attached to the front of old ships."

Wishbone, Joe, and David spent a few moments admiring the mermaid. Then they spent about fifteen minutes examining every inch of the basement. They found no other objects, and nothing that could be a secret passageway into the house.

"This basement sure is creepy," Joe said, "but it's clear of intruders."

About an hour later, the four humans and one dog met in the parlor. Every single window and door, except the front door, of the house had been taped. Every square inch of the house had been checked. No one had found any sign of a person or any sign of a secret passageway that led into the house.

"I hope we haven't missed anything," Wishbone told his friends. "But with this house, you can never be completely sure."

"Okay. Now let's go and question our suspects," Wanda said.

The humans put on their jackets in the entrance hall. Wishbone already had his outerwear on. Then the dog led the way out the front door. David placed a strip of tape across the crack where the front door met the door frame, on the outside.

"We'll check this tape when we come back," David explained. "I'm putting this piece on the outside so we won't tear it ourselves when we open the door."

The group walked toward their rental car, which was parked in front of the garage. Wishbone knew it was time to investigate the leading suspects—Teddy Lyman and Griffin and Scuffy, the two lobster fishermen.

It was a cool, cloudy, gray-skied day. A stiff breeze picked up. As the wind blew through some nearby trees, the dried leaves rattled like a pair of maracas.

While waiting for one of his friends to open the car door, Wishbone noticed something he hadn't seen before. Just beyond the trees, a short walk away, there was a black fence. On the other side of the fence, flat pieces of stone seemed to be growing out of the ground.

Uh-oh, Wishbone thought with a twitch of his

whiskers. *I know what that is. It's a graveyard. And it's practically right next door to us. Wow! Wanda really knows how to pick her property. That graveyard is probably the neighborhood hangout for all the local ghosts and witches and monsters and vampires and . . . Oh, stop it. You're scaring yourself for no reason!*

Chapter Nine

Wishbone glanced up at a sign that said: DEAD END. He was standing on a side street in the business district of Endicott with Joe, David, Sam, and Wanda. It was decided that Wanda and David would pay a visit to Mr. Lyman at his restaurant, while Joe and Sam went looking for the two lobster fishermen.

Wishbone gave his side a scratch. *I think I'll go to the restaurant, for the very simple reason that I'm hungry. It's been almost two hours since breakfast.*

Joe and Sam went one way; Wishbone, Wanda, and David went the other. Soon Wishbone's group came to Mr. Lyman's restaurant, The Portside Tavern. They opened the door and entered. It wasn't yet eleven o'clock and the restaurant was empty of customers.

"Mr. Lyman!" Wanda called out.

"Back here!" a voice boomed.

Wanda, David, and Wishbone passed through a swinging door and entered the kitchen. A gleaming metal counter stood in the center of the room. It was surrounded by an industrial-sized freezer, refrigerator, stove, and double sink. Boxes and sacks of food supplies lay scattered on the counter and floor.

There was also a big water tank in which a collection of slimy, greenish creatures lay clustered together. They moved, but only slightly. By the shelled bodies and scissor-like claws, Wishbone could tell they were lobsters.

I've never seen an aquarium in a kitchen, Wishbone thought. *It's a very nice decorating touch.*

"Hello, there," Lyman greeted the group, just as jolly as he had been the previous day. "Come right on in. I'm cooking up my world-famous bisque—best soup you'll ever taste. So tell me, how are you folks enjoying your stay in Endicott?"

"Oh, just fine," Wanda said. "Is there any reason we *shouldn't* be enjoying our stay?"

Lyman, the big man with the wavy red hair, was by himself in the kitchen. He went to the stove to check a huge kettle. From the steam and the smell, Wishbone knew it contained boiling water. Next to the kettle, some kind of tempting tomato sauce was simmering in a pot.

Wishbone licked his chops.

"Well, Endicott's an odd place," Lyman said, sprinkling a spicy-smelling powder into the pot. "Either you love it, or you don't. And I'm not so sure that you folks are loving it."

"Why shouldn't we love it?" Wanda asked directly.

"In a way, Endicott has always missed the boat," Lyman went on. "Portsmouth edged it out as the big shipping port in the state. Our fishing industries never grew as big as they should have. The shipbuilding yards never located here. It's never been a popular tourist spot.

It's just not a town people have taken to easily. Myself, I wouldn't live anywhere else. The people are a bit gruff, and the weather can get mighty rough, and there's not much in the way of entertainment or culture, but I—"

"I know what you're doing," Wanda said, suddenly annoyed. "You're trying to make me think I won't like this town. And you're doing it so I'll sell you Hathaway House. But you can just save your breath, Mr. Lyman. I like to make up my own mind about things, thank you very much."

"Maybe you're cut out to live in New Hampshire, after all," Lyman said with a hearty laugh. "Nobody values independent thinking more than the good people of this state. Our state motto is 'Live Free or Die.'"

Wishbone glanced over at the stove. "Say, Lyman, if you have some food around here that needs testing, I'm only too happy to help out."

Mr. Lyman was too busy to pay any attention to this request. Wishbone figured he would try again in a few minutes.

David stepped forward. "Mr. Lyman, if Hathaway House is really haunted, *who* do you think would be haunting it?"

"Oh, there's always been talk that it's the ghost of a young lady," Lyman said. "They say she was murdered in the house many years ago. Hope Hathaway, I think her name was."

Lyman was speaking matter-of-factly, but Wishbone wondered if he was really trying to frighten the Oakdale visitors.

"Did Homer Hathaway think the house was haunted?" David asked.

Lyman picked up a long wooden spoon, which he

used to stir the mixture in the pot. "Oh, yes. Homer was sure of it. He talked about all sorts of strange things going on in that house. Doors opening and closing by themselves. Strange smells and sounds. Sudden cold spots. That kind of foolishness. But, listen, Homer had a very lively imagination. Why are you folks asking about this? You haven't seen a ghost, have you?"

"No, of course we haven't," Wanda said, watching Lyman carefully. "We were just curious about the rumors."

Lyman pointed the wooden spoon at Wanda. "I really do want that house, Wanda. It would be the best spot in town for my sister's bed-and-breakfast. If you suspect the house is haunted, you'll never be comfortable there, so you may as well sell it. And even if it *is* haunted, well, by gosh, I still want it!"

"I might refuse to use the house, but I still don't think I'd sell it," Wanda said. "I believe Homer wanted it to stay in the family."

"Then I'll just buy it from whatever other relative ends up with it," Lyman said. "But I'd much rather give my money to you, Wanda. I'll tell you right now, I'm thinking of offering a very good price."

Hmm . . . Wishbone thought with interest. *A very good price. Let's see . . . That could buy . . . well, plenty of bones and chew toys.*

"Some extra money would come in handy right now," Wanda said, mostly to herself. "The newspaper office needs some new equipment, and I could do some real good for all the Oakdale charity organizations."

Lyman went to the lobster tank and pulled out a wiggling lobster with his bare hands. "Give my idea some good deep thought, Wanda. Then, please, make sure you get in touch with me before you leave town Monday morning. Will you promise to do that?"

"I'll do that," Wanda said, obviously thinking about the money.

"Now," Lyman said, carrying the lobster toward the huge kettle, "let me show you the secret behind a really excellent lobster bisque."

Wishbone watched in horror. *Wait! Those lobsters aren't here just for decoration. They're here for . . . soup! And I think some of them are about to go for a swim in that boiling water. I'd just as soon miss that!*

Wishbone went to a screen door at the back of the kitchen, pushed it open with his muzzle, and stepped outside. He found himself in an alleyway. Smelly, industrial-sized trash containers from the restaurant stood by a wall. Some of the smells were good, while some weren't.

Wishbone noticed a bulldog sitting across the alley. He was a squat fellow with a smushed-in face.

I wonder if this bulldog might know something about that mysterious black cat. As far as I'm concerned, that cat is on our suspect list, too.

Wishbone walked over to the bulldog. "Hello there, good sir."

The bulldog watched Wishbone carefully with its bugged-out eyes.

"Say, do you happen to know a black cat here in town?" Wishbone asked. "Fur, black as coal. Eyes, a very evil greenish-yellow."

The bulldog said nothing.

"You see," Wishbone continued, "I've been staying in Hathaway House with some friends of mine, and some funny stuff has been going on in there. I was wondering if this black cat might have anything to do with it. For example, do you know if this cat might have any kind of connection to some local witches?"

The bulldog remained tight-lipped. If it knew something, it wasn't talking about it.

"What's the matter?" Wishbone joked. "The cat got your tongue?"

The bulldog gave Wishbone a glare, as if to say "Don't go nosing into that black cat's business. Not if you know what's good for you."

Wishbone could see he would get no cooperation from the bulldog. After giving a farewell nod of his muzzle, he wandered to the end of the alley to see who else was in the neighborhood.

He caught sight of Joe and Sam walking down a side street. Wishbone raced over to them to see if they could use any of his expert detective skills.

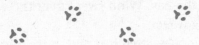

"Good to see you," Joe told Wishbone as he and Sam continued walking.

Joe was keeping a sharp lookout for the lobster fishermen, Griffin and Scuffy. The boy was determined to prove that Hathaway House was *not* haunted.

Though Joe no longer believed in ghosts, the thought of them still gave him the creeps.

For years, Joe had been afraid of ghosts. He had even convinced himself that an abandoned house in Oakdale, the old Murphy house, was haunted. He didn't even like to go near the place. This used to surprise Joe's friends because, in other ways, Joe was very brave. He always played courageously on the basketball court, and he never hesitated to stand up for what he believed was right. These leadership qualities had helped Joe become one of the captains of his high school's junior-varsity basketball team.

But last Halloween, Joe had discovered that the Murphy house was "haunted" by nothing more than a stray cat. This knowledge had set Joe free from his fear of ghosts. Since then he had come to realize that ghosts existed only in horror stories. Joe really wanted to keep it that way.

A few steps later, Joe, Sam, and Wishbone came to the bay. The inner part of the bay formed a natural harbor, around which spread the downtown area of

Endicott. There were far more businesses and homes in this part of town than elsewhere. The town had obviously grown out of the shipping and fishing opportunities provided by the bay. Wind swept over the water, stirring up the rolling waves.

Several docks stretched out into the water. Their wooden surfaces had turned rough and gray from the constant sun and damp sea air. A variety of boats were tied up at the docks—sailboats with dangling ropes and bare masts, boxy-shaped fishing boats that had seen better days, and a few elegant yachts. On one of the docks lay a collection of old wooden cages that Joe recognized as lobster traps.

Hearing a loud squawk, Joe suddenly saw a seagull swoop right by him, riding the wind seaward.

Joe waved to a group of older men who were sitting on benches. He imagined them to be salty fellows, swapping tall tales about their adventures at sea.

Then Joe turned to see a beat-up pickup truck rumbling its way along the docks ahead. When the truck turned a corner, Joe glimpsed Scuffy in the passenger's seat.

"That's them!" Joe exclaimed.

Joe raced after the truck as if he were hot on the heels of an opposing basketball player. The docks and boats and warehouses whizzed by in a blur. Joe passed an assortment of tarp-covered boats that rested on metal stands. They were being stored away for the coming cold season. Pouring on more speed, Joe turned the corner, following in the truck's path.

To the left, Joe saw the truck driving along Front Street. He charged after the vehicle, his legs and heart

pumping with fierce determination. Joe was getting close enough to yell to the passengers.

Suddenly, the truck jerked to a stop. Both doors flew open. Griffin and Scuffy leaped to the ground and rushed toward Joe, who was near the truck.

"What are you chasing after?" called Griffin, the one with the scraggly blond hair and earring.

"Yeah—what?" growled Scuffy, the short one with the eyebrow scar and droopy moustache.

Joe held up his hands. "I was just—"

"You wouldn't be trying to swipe some lobsters off our truck, would you?" Griffin said, showing a fist at the end of a muscular arm. "There used to be a guy around here who did that all the time. We set him straight, though."

"No, I promise I wasn't trying to steal lobsters off your truck," Joe said, trying to catch his breath.

Joe turned, seeing that Sam and Wishbone had just about caught up with him. They were both breathing hard, keeping their eyes on the fishermen.

"What's on your mind, out-of-towners?" Griffin said, unclenching his fist.

"We . . . uh . . . just wanted to say hello," Joe said, realizing that he was coming up with a lame excuse. "It looks like you guys are back to work today."

"Yeah, we just got a job delivering lobsters for Lucky, a fellow fisherman we know," Griffin replied. "Right now, we're bringing lobsters to this market here. Good thing, too. The last few days we've been doing nothing, on account of our boat being fixed."

Joe noticed the truck was parked in front of a food market. He also saw that the back of the truck held a big tank filled with water and live lobsters. Griffin and Scuffy were busy today. But if they hadn't been busy yesterday, Joe figured, that would have given them time to pull some pranks at Hathaway House.

"Did you folks see anything spooky in your house?" Scuffy said with a sneer.

"No, we didn't see anything spooky," Sam said in a casual way. "Not a single thing."

Scuffy climbed onto the back of the truck. He began pulling the greenish lobsters from the tank and putting them in a big plastic bucket. Joe could see that the lobsters' claws were kept shut with rubber bands. Griffin sat down on the truck's back fender.

"If there is a ghost in Hathaway House," Joe said, watching the fishermen closely, "who do *you* think it might be?"

Griffin began scratching his ear with a wooden matchstick. "Some say it's the ghost of a young lady. Her name was Hope Hathaway. She lived . . . oh . . . over a hundred years ago. One night she was all alone in the house, just minding her business. But she wasn't really alone, you see. Someone had sneaked into the house. And this person, well . . . he murdered her. Killed her dead."

Joe didn't know if the story was true or not, but hearing it gave him a brief shiver.

"Who was the murderer?" Sam asked.

"No one really knows for sure who it was," Griffin said, tossing his matchstick onto the ground. "That's the mystery of it."

"Some say she was murdered by a boyfriend she had turned away," Scuffy said, pulling a pair of lobsters out of the tank.

"Others say she was murdered by pirates," Griffin added.

Scuffy raised the two wiggling lobsters into the air. "And some say she was murdered by a pair of runaway lobsters!"

Griffin and Scuffy broke into a fit of laughter, as if this was the world's funniest joke. Joe could see that the two fishermen liked to tease almost as much as they liked to act tough.

"Well, thanks for all your help," Joe said politely to the two men.

As Griffin and Scuffy continued laughing, Joe, Sam, and Wishbone turned around and walked in the opposite direction. When they got to the next block, they met Wanda and David, who were just coming out of an old-fashioned candy shop.

As the group strolled down Front Street, they chewed small pieces of saltwater taffy and compared notes. After the morning's interviews, it seemed that all the original suspects were still in the running. Griffin and Scuffy seemed as if they might be mean enough to scare the Oakdale out-of-towners just for the fun of it. Teddy Lyman seemed very determined to buy Hathaway House, which would give him a good reason to scare Wanda into selling it.

Joe also found it interesting that both the fishermen and Mr. Lyman had mentioned that Hope Hathaway might be the ghost. This seemed to make the idea that Hathaway House was haunted just a little more believable. But then . . . Joe knew there couldn't possibly be a real ghost in Hathaway House.

"Let's explore the town a bit before we head back to

the house," Wanda suggested. "If one of these people we've just met with is trying to scare us, maybe they'll see now that we Oakdale folks don't scare so easily. We can stop for lunch in about an hour or so. Anybody have an idea of what they want?"

"Anything but lobster," David declared.

"Agreed," Joe and Sam said together.

Chapter Ten

After a terrific lunch of pizza and a few hours of sightseeing, Wishbone and his friends returned to Hathaway House. It still seemed to Wishbone that the front windows, shutters, and door on the gray clapboard house formed a face. In fact, a certain droop to some of the lower shutters made the house now seem to be frowning.

David checked the strip of tape he had placed on the front door. It was still there, exactly as he had placed it.

The group went inside, then split up to give the house a good checking over. After twenty minutes, they met in the parlor. Not one strip of tape had been pulled up, and there was no sign of anyone hiding in the house.

"For now," David announced, "the coast is clear."

Everyone settled in for some afternoon leisure activity. Sam sat in the parlor rocking chair, reading *The House of the Seven Gables*. David set his laptop computer on the parlor's coffee table and played a computer game. Joe stretched out on the sofa, watched the game, and tried to figure out how it worked. Wanda sat at the desk in the study, writing some letters.

Wishbone lay on the Oriental rug near the fireplace. He was trying to relax. But he couldn't shake the feeling that the house was just waiting to spring its next surprise.

In less than half an hour, it came.

Wishbone heard tires crunching on the gravel driveway. This was followed by footsteps and a few sharp raps at the front door.

"I'll get it," Wanda said, heading for the door.

Wishbone got to his feet, ready to rush to Wanda's side to protect her.

After looking through a peephole in the door, Wanda opened it.

Standing on the porch was a woman, her body wrapped in a black cloak that flapped in the breeze. Her gray hair was tied up neatly at the back of her head. She wore glasses with lenses that were shaped somewhere between a circle and a square. She was perhaps in her sixties or seventies. Wishbone wasn't sure whether she looked like a gigantic flying bat or a schoolteacher.

"Hello," Wanda said politely to the woman. "How may I help you?"

"Is Mr. Homer Hathaway at home?" the stranger asked.

"No, I'm afraid he's not," Wanda replied. "Are you a friend of his?"

"No, I never met the man. However, may I inquire where he is?"

"Actually . . . he has passed away."

The woman frowned. "Oh, how unfortunate."

"May *I* help you with something?"

"Who are you?"

109

"I'm a relative of Mr. Hathaway's. My name is Wanda Gilmore. Homer Hathaway has left the house to me in his will."

"I see," the woman said, looking Wanda over. "Do you suppose I might come in?"

"Uh . . . well . . . of course you may," Wanda said, opening the door wider. "Here, let me take your coat . . . I mean cloak."

Wanda helped the woman take off her cloak, which she hung up in the entrance hall. Under the cloak, the stranger wore a very plain skirt and blouse.

"These are my friends," Wanda said, leading the woman into the parlor. "Joe, Sam, and David. The furry fellow is Wishbone."

I wish she would stop calling me "the furry fellow," Wishbone thought with annoyance.

Each of the kids gave the elderly woman either a wave or nod.

She looked from person to person, as if memorizing their faces. "It is an honor to meet all of you. I am Miss Isabella Bridgewater."

"Have a seat, Miss Bridgewater," Wanda said, gesturing at the chairs. "Tell us what brings you here."

Miss Bridgewater looked around the parlor, her eyes lingering on each of the portraits. Finally, she sat in one of the armchairs, keeping her back as straight as an ironing board. Everyone gathered around, giving the woman their full attention.

"I am a parapsychologist," Miss Bridgewater stated.

"What's that?" Wishbone whispered to David. "A psychologist who works with parachutes?"

"What's a parapsychologist?" Joe asked.

"Parapsychology," Miss Bridgewater explained, "is a field of study that deals with matters that fall outside the limits of the so-called normal sciences. You know—things that cannot be explained by traditional scientific reasoning."

"You mean the supernatural," David said, sounding doubtful.

"I don't care for that word," Miss Bridgewater said. "It implies that people like myself are practicing black magic. We are scientists."

"That sounds like quite an interesting profession," Wanda commented.

"My specialty is ghosts," Miss Bridgewater continued. "I am a 'ghost investigator.' Sometimes we are known as 'ghost hunters.'"

Hmm . . . this lady sure doesn't look like a ghost hunter. Then, again, I don't believe I've ever met one.

"Is this a coincidence or what?" Sam whispered to David. "Her coming right at this time."

"Maybe it's not a coincidence," David said quietly.

David could be right. If someone is playing a prank on us, this Bridgewater lady could be a part of the prank. I think I'll keep a really close watch on her.

"Do you have a degree or license, or anything?" David asked Miss Bridgewater.

"I have a master's degree in psychology," Miss Bridgewater said. "I have also been a member of the American Society for Psychic Research for quite some time."

Wishbone couldn't help staring at Miss Bridgewater's glasses. The lenses were so thick that the woman's eyes appeared to be large unidentified objects floating in a sea of clear liquid.

"So, Miss Bridgewater," Wanda said cheerfully, "what brings you to Hathaway House?"

"My research focuses on hauntings in the New England region," Miss Bridgewater said, sounding very scientific. "For years, I have heard that Hathaway House was haunted, and so I have wanted to investigate it. I called Homer Hathaway many times, requesting permission to do so. Each time he refused. He said he liked the spirits in his house and did not wish to see them upset by a professional investigator."

"So you never got to investigate the house?" Sam asked.

"No," Miss Bridgewater answered. "But tomorrow I will be investigating a hotel not too far from here. I thought I would swing by Endicott and see Mr. Hathaway in person. Since the man is no longer with us, that will obviously not be possible. However, perhaps you, Miss Gilmore, will allow me to investigate the house."

Wanda opened her mouth with surprise. "How did you know I was 'Miss' rather than 'Mrs.'?"

"It's because I noticed that you are not wearing a wedding band."

"Oh, yes, of course. How silly of me."

"This is perfect timing," Sam told Miss Bridgewater. "We think there might be a ghost in the house. Well . . . *I* think there might a ghost in the house. The others aren't quite so sure."

Miss Bridgewater lifted a finger straight in the air. "Ninety-nine percent of all places that people believe to be haunted are not really haunted at all. The so-called 'hauntings' are simply the result of pranks, fraud, odd natural phenomena, or overactive imaginations."

Wanda stood up. "I think I'd like some tea. Perhaps you should come along with me to the kitchen, Miss Bridgewater. Something very peculiar happened when I boiled water in a teakettle this morning. It boiled within seconds. Perhaps it will happen again."

Wishbone rose to all fours. *I wouldn't mind a nice cup of tea—especially if it comes with a nice snack.*

The whole group went to the kitchen. Miss Bridgewater insisted on examining the teakettle very carefully. Then she handed it to Wanda. Wanda filled the kettle with water, put it on the stove, and turned on the bluish flame.

Seconds later, the kettle blew its shrill whistle.

"It did it again!" Sam exclaimed.

"It sure did," Wishbone said, his ears twitching from the noise.

Wanda poured some steaming-hot water into a mug.

"This could be a trick from the show of a second-rate magician," Miss Bridgewater said, eyeing Wanda suspiciously. "I'll have you know, Miss Gilmore, that many homeowners fake the haunting of their own property—especially when they are considering selling the property. Often they believe they will get more money for it because of all the attention it would draw."

"So you think I faked that myself?" Wanda said, offended.

Miss Bridgewater's suspicious stare melted into a kindly smile. "I meet so many pranksters in my line of work. I'm sure, Miss Gilmore, that you are an honest person. Please, forgive me for my comment."

"You're forgiven," Wanda said with a grudging nod.

Wishbone lifted his ears as he heard a whispered exchange among the kids.

"I don't know if I trust this lady," Joe whispered.

"That goes double for me," David whispered.

"I think I believe her," Sam whispered.

Wanda began boiling water in a pot. As the water heated up in the normal way, Wanda and the others told Miss Bridgewater about all the weird things that had happened in Hathaway House over the past twenty-four hours. They also mentioned their tape security system, their visits with the fishermen and Teddy Lyman, and the rumors about Hope Hathaway.

By the time the explanations were done, the water in the pot was boiling.

"Wanda," Wishbone called, "I'll take my tea with a slice of lemon, please. And . . . oh, yes, how about a nice sirloin steak on the side?"

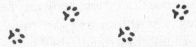

Everyone returned to the parlor and sat down. Wanda poured cups of tea, using the teapot and fine china from the dining room. Sam was so excited by Miss Bridgewater's presence that she burned her tongue with her first sip of tea. Sam was becoming more curious about ghosts by the minute.

"So is there a chance the house might be haunted?" Wanda asked anxiously.

Miss Bridgewater blew gently on her steaming tea. "It is possible that Hathaway House is haunted. However, it is also possible that you people are the victims of a cruel prank."

"Could it also be a poltergeist?" Joe asked. "I know those are similar to ghosts."

Sam noticed that Wanda and Joe were becoming more curious about ghosts, too. David just stared at Miss Bridgewater with a mistrustful look.

"What exactly is the difference between a ghost and a poltergeist?" Sam asked, leaning forward.

"A ghost aims its attention at one particular place," Miss Bridgewater explained. "For example, a home, hotel, battlefield, café, or graveyard. A poltergeist zooms in on one special person, usually someone between the ages of twelve and sixteen. Ghosts tend to be peaceful, while poltergeists are often mischievous or even dangerous."

Joe, David, and I are all between twelve and sixteen, Sam thought nervously.

"How are they dangerous?" Joe asked.

Miss Bridgewater wiggled, as if she had just seen a rat scurry across the floor. "Oh, they can be very wicked creatures. They toss things around, they make things crash to the ground, they pinch, they bite, they strangle. They've even been known to . . . well, enough said."

"My, my," Wanda said, holding a hand to her chest. "I hope we don't have one of those around. What causes a poltergeist to focus on a person?"

"It's usually because the person is troubled in some way," Miss Bridgewater answered. "For reasons we can't explain, the worry in this person's mind attracts the poltergeist. Or, indeed, the worry may *create* the poltergeist."

The wind outside caused some distant part of the house to give a low creak.

"These poltergeists sound pretty creepy," Joe said with a shudder.

Wishbone crept closer to Joe.

Sam caught David rolling his eyes.

"I seriously doubt we are dealing with a poltergeist," Miss Bridgewater said. "Let me ask you this. Have any of you experienced this kind of thing before?"

Everyone answered no.

Miss Bridgewater fixed her magnified eyes on Sam. "If I'm not mistaken, Sam has been present for every bit of the unexplained activity."

"I guess that's true," Sam admitted.

With sudden worry, Sam wondered if there could be a poltergeist that was focusing on *her*.

The afternoon light was fading, causing the shadows of the parlor's furniture to stretch out. This gave the room an odd sense of motion. For a brief moment, Sam felt as if the wallpapered walls and the drapes were moving forward, inching closer to where she sat.

"Sam, do me a favor," Miss Bridgewater said. "See if you can make my teacup explode—without touching it."

It was the strangest request Sam had ever heard. Sam looked at Wanda, who nodded. Sam gave it a try. Staring hard at the cup, Sam focused all her thoughts on making the piece of china shatter.

Wishbone placed his paws gver his ears.

Nothing happened.

"Sorry," Sam said with a shrug. "Now, could you tell me why I was doing that?"

"Very often poltergeist victims have the power to move or break objects with their mind," Miss Bridgewater said. "It appears that you don't have this power. Sam, tell me something. Lately, have you been deeply troubled by anything?"

"I've been bothered by a few minor things," Sam confessed. "But basically, I'm a very happy person."

"She's telling the truth," Wanda said. "I happen to know that Sam is a very well adjusted girl."

"I'm glad to hear it," Miss Bridgewater said, giving Sam a warm smile. "I really don't think Sam—or any of you—is the victim of a poltergeist. If there is a spirit in the house, then it will most definitely be a ghost."

Sam sighed with relief.

"However," Miss Bridgewater continued, "I refuse to believe even that until I have seen absolute proof of the ghost."

"You and me both," David said under his breath.

"Miss Bridgewater," Wanda said, "I would very much like it if you would conduct an investigation of Hathaway House. I need to know if there is a ghost in here or not. If there is, well, then . . . I just may consider selling the place."

"Yes," Miss Bridgewater said, setting down her teacup, "I would be most pleased to investigate this house. Now, if you kind folks will excuse me, I have an appointment for dinner in the area. I will return here around nine o'clock. We shall conduct the investigation at that time. In the dark hours of night, we will have a much better chance of meeting a ghost."

Sam noticed the shadows in the room had grown even longer.

Chapter Eleven

The grandfather clock in the entrance hall sounded nine gongs. It was nine o'clock, almost time for the ghost investigation to start.

Wishbone had been so keyed up for the past few hours that he hadn't taken a single nap, and he had barely begged for any extra food during dinner. As Miss Bridgewater had suggested before she had left earlier, Wishbone and the others had given Hathaway House another thorough search, just to make sure that no one had sneaked inside. The search had turned up no sign whatsoever of an intruder.

The wind, however, made it seem as if some stranger *had* crept inside the house. It worked its way inside the house's wooden framework, making whispers and whooshes that sounded very much like those of a living creature.

Wishbone practically jumped out of his fur when he heard the knock at the front door.

Joe ran to answer the door. Miss Bridgewater stood

on the porch, wearing her black cloak and holding a well-worn black suitcase.

She looks as if she could have been blown in from that nearby graveyard, Wishbone thought, twitching his whiskers.

"Good evening," Miss Bridgewater said with a very pleasant smile.

Wishbone, Joe, Sam, David, and Wanda followed Miss Bridgewater into the dining room. Miss Bridgewater set her suitcase on a chair, then removed her cloak. Joe hung it in the entrance hall.

"This is my ghost-detecting equipment," Miss Bridgewater said, as she unlocked the suitcase. "Simple but effective tools of the trade."

David watched glumly as the suitcase was opened. During dinner, he had warned the others not to take Miss Bridgewater too seriously. David was convinced that she was a fake. In fact, he suspected that *she* was the one trying to make Wanda believe that Hathaway House was haunted. By now, Wishbone and the others were starting to believe Miss Bridgewater was the real thing.

"Can you show us some of the equipment?" Sam asked eagerly.

"Not only will I do that," Miss Bridgewater said in her schoolteacherly way, "but I will be asking all of you to assist me with this investigation."

"Oh, we'd be glad to help," Wanda said, seeming very interested.

Wishbone placed his front paws on the chair that held the suitcase. "Just tell us what you need us to do, and we'll do it."

Miss Bridgewater pulled a camera from the suitcase.

"This is a digital camera. Very often a ghost will appear in a photograph, even though the ghost may not be visible to the naked eye."

"Photography is my favorite hobby," Sam said, as she moved in close to examine the camera. "Why do you like to use a digital model?"

"When a photograph is developed by hand or machine," Miss Bridgewater said, "there is always a chance a speck of dust or something will end up on the negative. With a digital camera, the photograph bypasses the development stage, and therefore you have a better chance of getting a purer picture."

"Good point," Sam said.

Miss Bridgewater slipped a floppy disk into the camera, then handed it to Sam. "Perhaps you would be good enough to be our photographer. When I tell you when and where to shoot, take pictures of that exact spot. Just keep shooting until the camera is out of pictures. I've turned off the camera's automatic flash device. Even

121

though the room will be dark, it's better without the flash."

"Got it," Sam said, slipping the camera strap around her neck.

"And what will you be needing me to do?" asked Wishbone.

Miss Bridgewater pulled out a black object that was shaped something like a gun. "This is a thermal scanner. It measures temperature. Often ghosts will cause the temperature to drop in a certain part of a room. This is known as a 'cold spot.' Joe, perhaps you'd like to be the one to operate the scanner."

"How does it work?" Joe asked, taking the scanner.

"It's very simple," Miss Bridgewater explained. "When I give the word, point the scanner where I tell you and then push that button. Then call out the temperature reading to me. It will appear in red digits in that tiny window on the scanner."

"Easy enough," Joe said, doing a test run.

"All right," Wishbone told Miss Bridgewater, "now that Joe and Sam are all set, let's talk about my assignment."

Miss Bridgewater pulled out another black object. This one resembled a TV remote control. "This is an EMF meter. It measures electromagnetic fields. More often than not, a ghost carries with it a fair amount of electro-magnetism."

David was the only one sitting down. "I have one in my garage. It counts magnetism in mGs, which are also known as milli-Gausses. It's useful for certain experiments."

"Then you shall be in charge of the EMF meter," Miss Bridgewater said, handing it to David. "Just take a reading when and where I tell you to."

"Okay, fine," Wishbone said, quickly running out of patience. "David gets the EMF meter. Now, as far as my job is concerned—"

Miss Bridgewater pulled out a stopwatch. "This is an ordinary stopwatch. Wanda, start the watch and then stop it exactly when I tell you to."

"Is that all I do?" Wanda said, taking the stopwatch.

"No," Miss Bridgewater said. "If we detect a ghost, I want you to keep a careful watch on all parts of the room. You'll be in charge of making sure someone is not pulling a prank on us."

"I understand," Wanda said with a serious nod.

"Hey, Miss B.," Wishbone called out, "aren't you forgetting somebody here?"

Miss Bridgewater's manner shifted from that of a schoolteacher to that of a coach preparing the team for a big game. "Now listen to me. If a ghost does come to us, most likely it will remain in our presence for only a very short time. Therefore, we will need to perform our various tasks quickly. Stay alert, do not panic, and listen carefully to my instructions."

Wishbone stared hard at Miss Bridgewater. "For barking out loud, lady, how come everyone gets a job but me? I've got four good paws, not to mention the best ears and nose in the business!"

Miss Bridgewater knelt down to pat Wishbone's back. "There is one more tool that we will be using. It may be our most valuable piece of equipment. I'm speaking of Wishbone. Dogs are especially sensitive to ghostly presences. Should a ghost appear, Wishbone will probably be the first to know it."

"Thank you, thank you," Wishbone said, after giving

the lady a lick. "I can see you recognize talent when you come across it."

Miss Bridgewater pulled out two packs of matches, which she handed to David and Joe. "Light every single candle in the dining room and parlor. After you've done that, we will turn out the lights. Ghosts usually feel less shy about appearing when there is candlelight."

Joe went to light the many candles in the parlor, while David lit the eight candles on the candelabra in the dining room. When Joe and David were done, all the lights were turned off in both rooms.

Miss Bridgewater motioned to everyone with her hand, signaling for them to sit down. The humans took seats in the high-backed chairs around the dining room table. Wishbone parked on the floor. Miss Bridgewater pulled a small notebook and pen from her suitcase.

The room had turned very spooky. It was completely dark except for the flickering light given off by the candles. The outlines of the furniture and the designs on the wallpaper seemed to be moving, just barely. The darkness also brought a deep hush to the room. Even the wind had faded.

Wishbone felt his tail thumping against the floor. *I'm kind of nervous, and no ghost has even shown up yet.*

"Now, we simply wait," Miss Bridgewater said in a low voice. "With any luck, the ghost will sense that we wish for it to appear. It may choose to do so, or it may choose to avoid us. We may talk, but not too loudly. And, I'll warn you, sometimes ghosts don't like to appear when there is a ghost investigator present."

"I guess it's like humans not wanting to visit the doctor," Joe said quietly.

"Hey, if you think going to the doctor is bad," Wishbone said, "try visiting a vet. I never walk out of that place without getting a shot or two!"

"If the ghost does come," Sam asked, "will we be able to see it?"

"Probably not," Miss Bridgewater replied. "But we will sense its presence in other ways. It may be through a sound or a smell or something in motion."

Okay, time to turn on my own personal ghost-detecting equipment.

Wishbone searched the room with his eyes. He saw nothing but the room's shadowy shapes and the flickering candles.

He raised his ears high. He heard only the usual sounds of the old house.

He pointed his little black nose into the air. He smelled all the regular smells, as well as the leftover aromas of dinner. Wanda had turned out to be a surprisingly good chef. For the evening meal, she had thrown together a very tasty stew: a mixture of beef, broth, spices, carrots, potatoes, celery, onions, garlic, and—

Flowers? I don't remember any flowers being in the stew.

All the same, Wishbone's nose was picking up a sweet-springlike-flowerly scent.

"Hey, everyone," Wishbone whispered. "I think our ghost may have arrived."

No one seemed to hear the dog.

Wishbone didn't have time to waste, trying to get everyone's attention. He had to zero in on the ghost—and he had to do it quickly. Without even pausing to think about being afraid, Wishbone began following the flowery scent.

The ghost-detecting dog, with his senses on full alert, walked slowly out of the dining room.

Sam noticed Wishbone leaving the room. She wondered if he was sensing a ghost, or if he was just setting off after something of interest only to a dog.

"Let's follow the dog," Miss Bridgewater said, rising to her feet. "Walk softly and say nothing."

Everyone followed Wishbone across the entrance hall and into the parlor. All around the candlelit room, tiny glows burned through the darkness, as if they were little living figures. The portraits seemed to be watching everything from the shadows.

Wishbone went to the middle of the room, his nose sniffing, his tail bristling.

Sam smelled a flowery-sweet scent that reminded her of perfume.

Miss Bridgewater stood as still as a statue. Behind the thick lenses of her glasses, her eyes seemed to shine as brightly as the candles.

"Wanda, start the stopwatch," Miss Bridgewater whispered. "I believe the ghost is here. I smell lavender. It may be the ghost's favorite perfume, or it may simply be a flower the ghost likes."

Sam saw nothing unusual in the room. She heard only the low ticking of the stopwatch.

"Stay alert for my instructions," Miss Bridgewater said, jotting something in her notebook.

Everyone, including David, seemed on edge.

Very slowly, Miss Bridgewater moved around the

room, letting both of her hands float up and down in the air. She looked as if she were swimming in slow motion. The others kept their eyes glued on her every movement. Miss Bridgewater was trying to feel something of an invisible nature. After covering half of the parlor, Miss Bridgewater moved to the second half of the room near the front door.

Suddenly she stopped.

She moved her right hand up and down in one small area, testing it.

"Quickly!" Miss Bridgewater said in an excited voice. "Everyone notice where my right hand is. I believe the ghost is right about here. Sam, begin taking pictures. David, Joe, aim your instruments and proceed. Wanda, are you checking the room for pranksters?"

"Uh . . . well . . . I forgot to for a second," Wanda said with embarrassment. "But I'll start doing it right now."

Miss Bridgewater stepped back from the spot where she had been waving her hand. Remembering where it had been, Sam aimed her camera at the spot. Looking through the viewfinder, she saw only darkness and a few candle flames.

Try to keep cool, Sam thought, feeling the camera shake in her hands. *This isn't the time to freak out.*

Sam pushed a button on the camera. With a click, she shot the first picture.

Out of the corner of her eye, Sam saw Joe and David aiming their instruments at the spot. Sam continued to take pictures of the exact same spot.

"The thermal scanner reads sixty-five degrees," Joe whispered.

"Take a reading a few feet away," Miss Bridgewater instructed.

Joe moved the scanner to a different direction. "It reads seventy-one degrees. Could that first reading have been a cold spot?"

"It must be," Miss Bridgewater said, scribbling a note. "It's a drop of six degrees. David, what's your reading?"

David sounded surprised. "What do you know! The needle is wavering around eight mGs. There's a pretty heavy electromagnetic field in that spot."

Sam's heart was pounding almost as fast as she was snapping pictures.

"Wanda, do you see anything?" Miss Bridgewater asked, scribbling a note.

Wanda was wandering around the room. "So far, I don't see a sign of anything."

Sam kept snapping pictures.

"The electromagnetic field is beginning to fade," David whispered.

"So is the cold spot," Joe whispered.

Sam could smell the lavender scent fading, too.

"Spirit," Miss Bridgewater called out in a bold voice, "I am Isabella Bridgewater. I am here with Wanda Gilmore, the lady who has inherited this house. We welcome your presence. We mean you no harm. Would you give us a sign of who you are?"

There was no response.

Sam lowered the digital camera, having just finished shooting all the pictures on the floppy disk. She realized her trembling fingers were gripping the camera very tightly.

"Spirit, stay!" Miss Bridgewater called out. "I ask you to stay!"

Except for the ticking of the stopwatch, the room was silent.

Everyone stared at Miss Bridgewater, wondering what to do next. Miss Bridgewater stood perfectly still for a few moments. Finally, she said, "Wanda, stop the watch. Tell me what your reading is."

"Two minutes and twelve seconds," Wanda said, after stopping the watch.

"The ghost is gone," Miss Bridgewater said, jotting down a note. "But there is no doubt about it. There is, most definitely, a ghost in this house."

Miss Bridgewater switched on several lamps in the parlor.

Sam blinked as the artificial light filled the room. She discovered she was still gripping the camera, even though it was attached to a strap around her neck. Joe, Wanda, Wishbone, and even David looked as dazed as Sam felt.

Last night in my bedroom, the ghost seemed almost like part of a dream, Sam thought. *It feels a lot more real now that the others are here. This is soooo weird!*

Miss Bridgewater gave everyone in the room a comforting touch. "You may relax. Please do not be frightened. Everything is all right."

"I guess this equipment can't lie," Joe said, a slight tremble in his voice. "That must have been a ghost in here. David, what do you think?"

"Coolness and electromagnetism can be caused by any number of things," David said, glancing at Miss Bridgewater. "We still don't have definite proof that this was a ghost. I'm sorry to sound so doubtful."

Sam pulled the disk out of the camera. She knew the photos she had just taken were stored on the disk.

"What do you think the photos might show?" Sam said, handing the disk to Miss Bridgewater.

"Perhaps nothing," Miss Bridgewater said. "But they may show something like a hazy light or a swirl of mist. Occasionally, something more identifiable appears. We can look at the pictures right away. I always carry a laptop computer in my car for just that purpose."

Miss Bridgewater began walking toward the entrance hall, but David stopped her with his voice. "Don't bother, Miss Bridgewater. I have a laptop right here in the parlor. I have software to view photos."

David doesn't trust Miss Bridgewater to use her own computer, Sam realized. He must suspect that she can somehow fudge the pictures. I suppose it's good that David is so suspicious. He'll make sure Miss Bridgewater doesn't get away with anything dishonest.

"Very well," Miss Bridgewater said, returning to the others. "David, you may set up the pictures for us."

David knelt on the floor, right beside his laptop computer, which was on the coffee table. He booted up the computer. Then he took the disk from Miss Bridgewater and inserted it into the laptop's disk drive.

Everyone gathered around the computer, including Wishbone. The wind had picked up again, sending shuddering noises through the house's framework. Soon the computer was all set to go.

David clicked on the disk icon. Within seconds, twenty "thumbnail" photographs appeared on the screen in rows of five. Each photo was about one and a half by two inches in size.

Sam ran her eyes carefully over the photos. All the photos in the first two rows looked exactly the same—

darkness, with a few background blurs of candlelight. When Sam examined the photographs in the third row, she saw something different. One of them contained a cloudy spot of grayness. Sam finished looking at the other photos, but none of them showed the cloudy spot.

"Click on that one," Sam told David, pointing at the spotted photo.

David clicked on the photo. A white box, about three by five inches in size, appeared on the computer screen. Gradually, the colors and shapes of the photograph began to fill the box.

The spot of grayness was now larger and less cloudy. Sam stared at the spot very hard. It seemed to be the image of a human face, drawn with swirls of smoke. There were eyes and eyebrows and a nose and a mouth, which seemed as if it might be smiling. Sam couldn't tell if it was the image of a man, woman, or child, but it was, very clearly . . . *a face*.

Sam's heart skipped a beat.

Wanda gasped.

Joe took a deep breath.

"This is one of the most remarkable images I've ever seen," Miss Bridgewater said, moving in so that she could get a better look. "That is, indeed, the photographic image of a ghostly face!"

"I wish I could see the face better," Sam said, leaning closer to the screen. "But if David makes the image larger, it will just get blurry. This is the best we can do."

Joe turned to David. "What do you say now, David?"

David looked at Joe, and his face seemed frozen with amazement. "I think . . . I think . . . I'm staring into the face of . . . something from another world."

David's response seemed to make it official for Sam. She felt a fluttering sensation in her stomach, as if a hundred butterflies had just been set free in there.

I just took a picture of a ghost! I can't believe it—but I have to believe it, because the visual evidence is right there staring at me!

Sam, Joe, and David kept their eyes locked on the photograph, as if some unknown force refused to allow them to pull their eyes away. Even Wishbone was staring at the picture, his front paws resting on the coffee table.

A sudden gust of wind gave the house a rough shake.

Wanda began pacing around the room like a confused mother hen. "Oh, my gosh! We're staying in a house that is really haunted! Maybe we should pack our things and leave this very minute."

"Calm down," Miss Bridgewater told Wanda.

"But I'm responsible for Joe, Sam, and David," Wanda said, her voice rising to a strained pitch. "I assured their parents I would watch them as if they were my own kids. I must think of their safety!"

"I beg you to calm down," Miss Bridgewater said, placing a hand on Wanda's arm. "Listen to me—all of you. I don't know who this ghost is or why it is here. But this spirit has made no attempt to harm us. As I said before, ghosts are almost never dangerous."

"Are you sure about that?" Joe asked.

"Yes, I am," Miss Bridgewater said firmly. "People are never seriously injured by ghosts unless they panic. Then they're likely to fall down or go into a state of shock—or who knows what. If we stay calm, everyone will be just fine. That is a promise!"

"All right," Wanda said, rubbing her hands together nervously. "We will all remain calm. But I have a very important request. Miss Bridgewater, could you possibly spend the night in Hathaway House, right here with us—*and this ghost?*"

"I would be delighted to spend the night," Miss Bridgewater said, giving Wanda's shoulder a friendly pat. "Now, let's just settle down and have ourselves a relaxing evening."

Sam continued staring at the ghostly face, feeling anything but relaxed.

Chapter Twelve

Sam watched flames leaping and dancing in the fireplace. She was sitting on the parlor floor, stroking Wishbone's back. Joe, David, Wanda, and Miss Bridgewater were seated nearby.

Miss Bridgewater had instructed that a fire be made and popcorn popped. She felt that doing these normal things would help to soothe everyone's nerves. Surprisingly, her plan had worked. It had been less than a half an hour since the ghost investigation had ended, and already everyone was somewhat calmer.

"This may be a dumb question," Joe said, reaching for the overflowing popcorn bowl. "But how do ghosts manage to . . . uh . . . well . . . how do they appear?"

As Miss Bridgewater spoke, the fire reflected in her eyeglass lenses. "I've been studying ghosts for the past twenty-four years, yet I still don't know the answer to that question. Somehow, the spirits of certain dead persons are able to exist in the natural world. How it's done, well . . . that remains an unsolved mystery."

David shook his head slowly. "I just don't see how it's possible. And yet, tonight I saw proof."

"Do we know *why* ghosts appear?" Sam asked.

"Yes, that question is much easier to answer," Miss Bridgewater replied. "There are four major reasons that cause a dead person to appear in ghostly form. I like to call these reasons the four *r*'s: resolve, revenge, refusal, and renovation."

"What do they mean?" Wanda asked.

"'Resolve' means a ghost is trying to make peace with its death," Miss Bridgewater explained. "This happens to the spirit of a person who has died in a very sudden manner, such as a car crash. The person was totally unprepared for death, and he or she needs some final solution before being able to accept it."

"That could be the case with Hope Hathaway," Joe pointed out. "*If* she really was murdered in the house."

"'Revenge' means the ghost is seeking revenge on a person who has wronged him or her in life," Miss Bridgewater continued. "Often this applies to the spirit of a person who has been murdered. Sometimes the ghost will continue to seek revenge on the wrongdoer's ancestors, or perhaps just anyone the spirit can lay its ghostly presence on. Let me say, however, that the ghost is rarely able to cause a person real harm."

"I suppose that explanation could apply to Hope Hathaway, too," David put in.

Sam found this information fascinating. A few days ago, she wasn't sure that she believed in ghosts. Suddenly, there she was, staying in a house with a genuine ghost and learning all about ghosts from an expert in the field. Sam hadn't even realized that there *were* ghost experts.

"The first two reasons are the most common," Miss Bridgewater said. "Ninety percent of these spirits that refuse to leave this life have suffered some kind of a very sudden or unpleasant death."

"Tell us about the other two reasons," Joe said, resting a foot on the coffee table.

"'Refusal' means that the ghost simply cannot bear to let go of life," Miss Bridgewater said. "I find this to be an especially touching reason."

"I can see how someone might feel that way," Sam said, glancing at the fire.

"'Renovation' means the ghost has come to protest some kind of physical change in a building or house," Miss Bridgewater continued. "The ghost wants the place left exactly as he or she remembered it."

Sam glanced at the portraits in the room. *I wonder if my friends and I are unwelcome here. We spent a lot of time today searching for an intruder. But maybe the ghost thinks of us as the intruders.*

"It's interesting how ghosts have such complicated feelings," Wanda said, taking a handful of popcorn.

Miss Bridgewater showed a smile that made Sam relax. "Most people fail to realize that ghosts are simply human beings in another form. They are capable of showing all the feelings known to any of us. They are people, not monsters."

"Do you believe in other supernatural things?" Joe asked. "You know, like vampires, werewolves, and witches."

Wishbone raised his ears high. "Yeah, what about witches? I could really use an expert opinion on the subject of witches."

"Vampires, werewolves, and evil witches are fine for novels, movies, and comic books," Miss Bridgewater said with a chuckle. "But you can be quite sure that they do not exist in real life."

"Boy, I'm glad to hear you say that," Wishbone told Miss Bridgewater. "I'll tell you why. I keep seeing this black cat, and I was starting to think that it might be some kind of a witch. I even thought it might be causing some of the weird stuff right here in Hathaway—"

Wishbone stopped in mid-sentence. He saw a pair of greenish-yellow eyes staring through the parlor window. At once, the dog knew that he was looking at the very thing he had been discussing—the black cat.

This may not be a coincidence, Wishbone thought, as the others continued talking. *Last night I saw the black cat staring at us. After that, weird things happened in the house. Just a little while ago, weird things happened in the house again. Right afterward, I'm seeing the black cat again. I don't care what you say, Miss Bridgewater. I think that cat might be a witch!*

The cat focused its frightening eyes right on Wishbone.

I know what I need to do. I need to have myself a chat with that cat.

Wishbone politely excused himself and trotted into the kitchen. He passed through the doggie door.

Once he was outside, a sharp wind brushed through Wishbone's fur. The nearby tree leaves rattled. With determination in his step, Wishbone trotted around to the front of the house.

The black cat turned and saw Wishbone approach. Just like a ballet dancer, the creature leaped off the windowsill and began slinking away.

Ha! Wishbone thought with pride. *One look at me, and you go running! I guess I showed you who—*

The cat wasn't gone, however. Just up ahead, there were two greenish-yellow eyes glowing through the night's darkness.

Uh-oh!

Wishbone stared at the eyes, becoming almost hypnotized by their power. The eyes seemed to be calling to Wishbone. The eyes seemed to say "Follow me. Follow me. Follow me . . . if you dare."

The eyes vanished as the cat disappeared into the night. Though Wishbone realized it might be a bad idea to follow the cat, he felt an overwhelming desire to do just that. He set his paws in motion.

Though it was very dark, Wishbone was able to stay on the cat's trail by following its scent. It was a gloomy, moonless, windy night, and there seemed to be not another soul on Earth. The black cat lured Wishbone along the dirt road that led away from Hathaway House—through a thick forest of trees, past a neighborhood of unlit houses, past a white church with a bell tower, and, finally, to the business district of Endicott.

Even though Wishbone was chasing the cat, he had the disturbing feeling that *he* was the one being chased.

The journey ended in the alleyway behind The Portside Tavern. Wishbone recognized the spot by the sight and smells of the restaurant's industrial-sized trash containers. What Wishbone saw next caused his tail to quiver with uneasiness.

The alley was crawling with cats, well over a dozen of them. Some were sleek and well groomed, some were shaggy. Some were big, some small. Some were solid, and others were striped or spotted. The colors ranged from black to gray to beige to orange to white, and there were all kinds of mixtures in between.

As the black cat joined the other felines, Wishbone lingered at the entrance of the alleyway. The cats were standing in a circle. They seemed to be gathered around something, but Wishbone couldn't see what it was.

This doesn't seem like regular cat activity, Wishbone thought with concern. *Cats lick their fur, lap up milk, stare at the walls, sleep even more than they lick their fur. But cats don't gather in circles doing . . . whatever these cats are doing.*

One of the cats made a mewing-moaning sound.

I have a feeling these aren't just regular cats. I have a feeling these are . . . witch-cats. What's it called when a group of witches get together to do their black magic? It's called . . . oh, yes, a coven. This could be a coven of witch-cats!

Several more cats joined together in a chorus of mewing-moaning noises. The sound was somewhere between a song and a chant. The dog's whiskers gave a shiver.

If these are witch-cats, what could they be doing? Casting a spell on someone? Brewing a caldron of lizards, gizzards, and snails? I need to know what these cats are up to.

Paw after paw, Wishbone silently crept ever closer to the circular cat coven. The cats were so busy with their activity that they didn't notice the approaching dog. A gust of wind blew, sending a tin can clanking across the alley. Wishbone was growing more and more alarmed by the second, but he forced himself to keep creeping forward.

An orange tabby cat, the fattest of the group, spun around. The cat released a terrifying hiss.

Wishbone froze in place. All of the other cats spun around.

The dog noticed the greenish-yellow eyes of the black cat focusing on him like a pair of headlights. The eyes seemed to say "You chose to follow me. Now you must pay for the choice you've made!"

Alarm ran through Wishbone's fur as if it were a jolt of electricity.

A scrawny, gray-striped cat opened its mouth, showing a set of what looked like razor-sharp fangs. The cat let out a snarling-hissing-roar that seemed to shoot straight out of the darkest depths of a nightmare.

You know what? Wishbone thought as he backed away, *I think I'd better get out of here. There's no telling what kind of spell or hex or curse these cats might put on me. And if something would happen to me, well, then, who would look*

after Joe, Sam, David, and Wanda? After all, I'm the house watchdog.

The dog turned quickly and ran out of the alleyway.

He peered through the darkness at the unfamiliar surroundings. Normally, Wishbone had an excellent sense of direction. But suddenly he wasn't sure which way he should go.

Those darned cats! They've gotten me all mixed up!

Finally, after losing precious time, Wishbone made his way back to Hathaway House. He passed through the doggie door and went straight upstairs to check on his friends.

Chapter Thirteen

David suddenly saw Wishbone. The dog was poking his muzzle through the doorway of the boy's second-floor bedroom. The terrier looked at David, glanced around the room, then left. David wasn't sure if Wishbone was looking for food, or whether he was just checking to see if everything was all right.

David was sitting on the floor, leaning against his bed. He and his friends had gone up to their bedrooms around midnight, a half hour ago. Since then, David had just been sitting quietly by himself, thinking.

David was stunned that he had been in the presence of what seemed to be a real ghost.

He looked at the Galileo thermometer, which hung on the wall. It was a glass tube that was two feet tall, inside of which five purple-colored spheres floated in a clear liquid. When the temperature climbed higher, the spheres sank lower. The room's temperature could be measured by looking at the lowest sphere. The famous Italian scientist Galileo Galilei had invented the device during the sixteenth century, after he had discovered that the chemical makeup of a liquid changed when there were changes in temperature.

David understood this principle. It was science. It could be explained by the logical laws of physics, chemistry, and math. David also understood how televisions worked and how the pull of the Moon affected the tides in the oceans.

But ghosts were a whole different ball game. Scientifically, they could not be explained. Their existence was supposed to be impossible. And yet, just a few hours ago, David had seen provable evidence that a ghost was in Hathaway House.

The wind whipped against the house.

David felt as if his mind were spinning in wild circles. The ghostly photograph forced him to rethink everything he thought he knew about the natural world. If he had been all wrong about ghosts, how many other things had he been mistaken about?

David knew that a good scientist always kept his mind open to new possibilities. For centuries, everyone had believed that the Sun revolved around the Earth. But Galileo had kept his mind open, and he had eventually discovered that, in fact, the Earth revolved around the Sun.

David decided that he would try to accept the fact that ghosts could exist in some form. And he would also try to learn as much as he could about them.

Having come to this conclusion, David felt a bit more at peace. Exhausted from the day, David climbed into his bed. He closed his eyes, hoping he would be able to fall asleep soon.

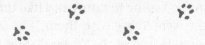

Sam was glad to have Wishbone at the foot of her bed. About an hour and a half ago, she had heard some noise on the second floor and realized it was the dog. Shortly after, he appeared at her door.

Sam heard two distant gongs of the grandfather clock on the first floor. It was two o'clock in the morning. The bedroom was dark, except for a small circle of light given off by the nightstand lamp. It sounded as if everyone else in the house was asleep. The wind had died down, giving only an occasional sad-sounding sigh.

For the past two hours, Sam had been reading *The House of the Seven Gables*. She had also managed to read throughout much of the day. Sam had moved rapidly through the book, and she was now only about sixty pages away from the end.

Sam glanced across the room at the antique music box. She wondered if it might play tonight. Surprisingly, she found herself half-hoping that it would.

After listening to Miss Bridgewater talk for several hours, Sam found the idea of a ghost less scary. First, Miss Bridgewater had made it clear that ghosts were not dangerous in most situations. Second, Miss Bridgewater had pointed out that ghosts were not monsters, but versions of people. In fact, they were spirits with very human problems. Sam also felt somewhat safe, knowing that Miss Bridgewater was spending the night in the house.

Sam buried her eyes and thoughts in *The House of the Seven Gables*. Even though nothing much happened for long stretches of the book, the story was holding Sam's attention. Sam had come to know and like the characters, almost as if she were living with them.

The gloomy House of the Seven Gables had become much more pleasant since the arrival of the sunny, young woman named Phoebe. She had even made friends with all the chickens that roamed around the back of the house. As Sam had guessed would happen, a romance had blossomed between Phoebe and Holgrave, the young daguerreotype artist who rented a room on the top floor of the house. Sam identified with Holgrave because he made daguerreotypes, an early form of photographs. He also lived in a top-floor room with a gable, as Sam was doing.

Hepzibah, the scowling lady who ran the house, had a shop on the ground floor of the house. There she sold penny candy and other small items. She also spent a lot of time looking after her brother, Clifford, the strange, childlike man. Clifford spent most of his days just gazing out a window, watching the activity on the street. Sam learned that Clifford had recently been released from a long term in prison. He had been found guilty of murdering a relative, even though he was really innocent.

The story took a creepy turn as Sam started reading the chapter called "The Scowl and the Smile."

Judge Jaffrey Pyncheon, a cousin of Hepzibah's, came to visit at the house. He was one of the most respected men in town, yet greed hid just beneath his constant smile. The judge wanted to speak with Clifford, believing that Clifford knew the location of some long-lost document. Hepzibah was afraid the judge would scare Clifford, but the judge demanded that Clifford be brought to speak with him.

Hepzibah went to get Clifford, but she couldn't find

him. When she returned to the parlor, she found Judge Pyncheon waiting patiently in a chair. Even though his eyes were wide open, the man was dead. His shirt was stained with blood.

Sam felt goose bumps rising all over.

The judge's ancestor, Colonel Pyncheon, had died in the exact same way about a hundred and fifty years earlier. Like his ancestor, Judge Pyncheon had done a few unfair things to his fellowmen. It seemed that the deaths of both Colonel Pyncheon and Judge Pyncheon might have been caused by Matthew Maule's curse—"God will give him blood to drink." To make matters even scarier, the dead judge was sitting right under a portrait of the dead colonel.

As Sam turned a page, she became aware of a rough, raspy, breathlike noise. It sounded something like Wanda's gargling, but worse.

Sam realized the sound was coming from somewhere very close to her room.

Sam's nervousness melted when she remembered that Miss Bridgewater was sleeping in the room just down the hall from her. It sounded like Miss Bridgewater was one of those people with a fairly loud snore.

That's a relief, Sam thought with a smile.

Sam returned to her story. Hepzibah finally found Clifford, and the two of them quickly fled the house. Hepzibah feared that Clifford might be accused of murdering Judge Pyncheon, even though she knew her brother would never do such a thing.

Then the book's author, Nathaniel Hawthorne, did something Sam had never come across before in a book. He took the reader inside the thoughts of the dead man.

Judge Pyncheon sat in his favorite chair, staring at a corner of the room, not moving a muscle. Even though he was no longer alive, the judge thought about all the appointments that he had scheduled for the day. He needed to go to his local bank, attend a property auction, purchase a racing horse, and visit the doctor because of his recent breathing problems. That evening he planned to go to a banquet. There he expected that the town's leaders would declare him the man most qualified to become the state's next governor.

And yet, the judge didn't budge from his chair because, of course . . . he was dead. As the day drifted on, no one entered the house. The parlor remained completely silent, except for the ticking of the judge's pocket watch. The shadows in the room grew ever longer. Then came twilight, then darkness.

At midnight, as moonbeams slanted through the window, the judge imagined his ancestor, Colonel Pyncheon, entering the room. He was the man who, many years ago, had stolen the land for the house by having Matthew Maule hanged for practicing witchcraft.

Then other Pyncheon ancestors entered the moonlit room. All the ghostly figures gathered around the portrait of Colonel Pyncheon that hung on the wall. They stared at it, puzzled, as if trying to solve a mystery. Judge Pyncheon imagined himself rising from the chair and staring at the portrait, a frown on his face.

It seemed that there was some secret attached to the portrait—a secret that only the ghosts knew about.

Finally, dawn arrived. The judge's pocket watch stopped ticking. Judge Pyncheon remained in his chair, eyes open, still thinking . . . but no longer alive.

Well, that was weird, Sam thought, setting the book on the bed.

The chapter had turned Sam's thoughts back to ghosts. Sam found herself to be very curious about the ghost who haunted Hathaway House. The lavender scent made Sam think that it was probably a woman, but she realized a man could also like lavender flowers.

Sam thought about the four "r's," Miss Bridgewater's reasons for why a ghost would feel the need to haunt a place. Sam wondered which of those four reasons might apply to the spirit that was in Hathaway House.

As if responding to Sam's thoughts, the wind chimes sounded their clinking tones.

Sam turned to see the metal tubes moving slightly. Yet, like the previous night, the window was shut, and Sam felt no breeze by the bed.

I think the ghost is back.

Sam felt her heartbeat increasing. However, she

wasn't nearly as afraid of the ghost as she had been the night before.

Wishbone woke up, startled by the sudden noise. The terrier glanced at the wind chimes, and then he looked at Sam.

"Come here," Sam whispered to the dog.

Wishbone went to Sam and lay beside her. Sam ran a soothing hand across the dog's back, trying to make them both feel safe.

At least I think *we're safe,* Sam thought, still watching the wind chimes. *Should I call for Miss Bridgewater? I think I'd rather not. It might scare the ghost away. Things are really taking a strange turn. Now I'm worried that I'll scare the ghost, instead of the other way around.*

As the wind chimes settled back into silence, Sam heard the soft notes of the antique music box. Sam saw that the lid of the music box was open, even though it had been shut a short time ago.

The ghost is definitely here!

Sam realized that the melody played by the music box was familiar. She shut her eyes, trying to recall what it was. Finally, the answer came to her.

The melody was an aria, or individual song, from an opera. The aria was titled "Nessun Dorma," which was Italian for "No One Shall Sleep." The tune was so hauntingly beautiful that it seemed to lift Sam's heart. Sam's mother liked opera, and Sam had frequently heard her humming this exact melody.

Sam had gotten used to not living with her mother, but she still missed her company. Sam's parents' divorce was just another one of those complicated things that had been part of the package of growing up. Sam reminded herself to get in touch with her mother as soon as she returned to Oakdale.

As the beautiful melody continued, Sam felt more and more sympathy for the ghost.

How could I not like someone who enjoys the sounds of wind chimes and a music box? Sam thought, opening her eyes. *It must be the ghost of a friendly, decent, artistic person. But who is it? Who in the world could it be?*

Before she realized what she was doing, Sam whispered to the room, "Who are you? Tell me, please. I'd like to know."

After a few more notes, the music box stopped its melody.

Once again, Sam whispered, "Who are you?"

Chapter Fourteen

SUNDAY

L ooking out a window, Wishbone watched a dark cloud float through the sky. It reminded him of a wandering soul.

The dog was sitting on the kitchen floor as Joe, David, Wanda, and Miss Bridgewater ate their breakfast of juice and fruit-topped cereal. The dog had finished his breakfast of dry kibble about ten minutes earlier, but he already felt hungry again.

Wishbone got up and walked over to Miss Bridgewater. "Gee, Miss Bridgewater, you sure are looking really beautiful, charming, and smart this morning. Say, how would you feel about sharing some of that cereal with your new pal, Wishbone?"

Miss Bridgewater was too wrapped up in the conversation to hear. She was telling the others about a haunted castle she had once visited in England. Joe, David, and Wanda were hanging on every word.

As Sam entered the kitchen, David said, "I see you're the last one to breakfast again."

"I hope that doesn't mean I have to eat rotten eggs," Sam said, covering a yawn.

"No," Wanda said with a welcoming smile, "but you can put some of this wonderful fruit on your cereal. It's all set out here on the table. Help yourself."

Sam took a seat at the table and fixed herself a bowl of cereal with fruit slices and milk.

"Gee, Sam," Wishbone said, walking over to the girl, "you sure are looking beautiful, charming, and smart this morning. Say, how would you feel about sharing some of that cereal with your old pal, Wishbone?"

Seeing the dog, Sam dropped a few pieces of cereal on the floor. Wishbone quickly crunched away at his immediately-after-breakfast snack.

Miss Bridgewater gave Sam a kindly look. "Were you visited by anyone last night, my dear?"

"Yes, I was," Sam said. "I heard the wind chimes and the music box, just the way I did the night before. It's weird, though. This time I felt pretty comfortable with the ghost."

"I was there, too," Wishbone offered. "In fact, that's probably why Sam wasn't so afraid. She knew that I would protect her if that ghost—or whatever it was—tried any funny business."

"Often people come to think of ghosts as friends," Miss Bridgewater said, after a sip of juice. "They treat them just as if they are real people. And that is just what they are."

"I'm really curious to know who this ghost is," Sam told Miss Bridgewater. "I even tried asking it, but I didn't get any answer. Is there anything I can do to discover the ghost's identity?"

"Yes, there is," Miss Bridgewater replied. "The most important thing is to learn as much about this house as possible. Who has lived here? What has happened here? And who would have a reason for haunting the house? Remember the four *r*'s I taught you?"

"Resolve, revenge, refusal, and renovation," Sam said, sounding like a good student.

"Exactly," Miss Bridgewater said with a nod.

Worry showed on Wanda's face. "I'd like to know a thing or two about this ghost myself. This is our third and last full day in the house, and I need to decide what to do with the place. Do I tell Mr. Whipple I'm not interested in taking it? Or do I take it but then turn around and sell it to Mr. Lyman? Or do I just keep the house for my own use, as I originally planned?"

Miss Bridgewater reached into her skirt pocket and pulled out a business card, which she handed to Wanda. "If you decide to keep Hathaway House, give me a call. Then I will come back and spend several days here. Hopefully, I will be able to determine exactly who the ghost is, and what he or she is after. Keep in mind that there may be even more than one ghost here. Most likely, I will bring a medium with me."

Wishbone's ears perked up. "Are you talking about steaks? That'll be great. And I don't care how they're cooked. Medium is fine, but so is medium-rare or well done. I'm not a picky eater."

"A medium is one of those people who conducts séances, right?" David asked.

Séances? Wishbone thought with confusion. *Oh, yeah, right—that's when a bunch of people sit around and try to contact the spirit of a dead person. I guess that Miss Bridgewater wasn't talking about steaks, after all.*

"Yes, mediums hold séances," Miss Bridgewater explained to the group. "They are people who are born with a special psychic ability. They can actually hear the voices of spirits, and very often the spirits can hear them. It's as if the medium is tuning into a radio station that operates on a sound level that only they can hear. It's quite a remarkable talent. Sometimes mediums are even hired by police departments in order to help solve the most puzzling murder cases."

"But you don't have that talent?" Joe asked.

"No. I usually locate the presence of a ghost by using purely scientific methods," Miss Bridgewater replied. "Mediums are much better at actually communicating with ghosts."

"Can ordinary people like us ever communicate with ghosts?" Sam asked.

"It happens now and then," Miss Bridgewater said, "especially if the ghost is eager to communicate. Indeed, if you would like to, the four of you could conduct your very own séance tonight."

"That might be really interesting," David said, lifting a spoonful of cereal. "Miss Gilmore, you have some experience acting as a medium."

Wishbone knew what David was talking about. The previous year, Wanda had conducted a séance when it was suspected that Joe's clubhouse was haunted. However, the "ghosts" in that case turned out to be a couple of mischievous kids.

"Yes, but that was different," Wanda pointed out. "I didn't really think there was a ghost in the clubhouse. But there *really* is a ghost in Hathaway House, and I don't consider myself qualified to deal with it."

"As I've said before," Miss Bridgewater noted, "I am certain the ghost is not dangerous. Wanda, I realize you are not a professional medium, but if you wish to lead a séance in here, I see no harm. Besides, tonight may be the perfect time to hold a séance."

"Why is that?" Joe asked.

Miss Bridgewater's eyes blinked behind her thick glasses. "Have you forgotten? Today is All Hallows' Eve, also known as Halloween. It's like the New Year's Eve of the spirit world. The ghosts should be out in all of their invisible glory."

Sensing something, Wishbone turned his head. The kitchen door closed just a few inches—all by itself. The others all saw it happen, too.

156

As Sam stared at the door, the others began bombarding Miss Bridgewater with questions.

"What physical substance do you think the ghost might be made of?" David asked.

"Are you sure the ghost isn't dangerous?" Joe asked.

"When do you think you might be able to come back to the house?" Wanda asked.

Wishbone came over to Miss Bridgewater and pawed at her leg. "I've got just a few more questions about witches. See, last night I saw—"

Miss Bridgewater wiped her mouth with a napkin, then got up from the table. "I'm afraid I will have to answer all of your questions another time. Wanda has my phone number. Right now, I'm late for an appointment at a haunted hotel in the western part of the state. Even though ghosts often live for centuries, they do not like to be kept waiting."

Miss Bridgewater laughed gleefully at the little joke she had made.

After helping the others clean up from breakfast, Sam went to the study. Since the night before she had been more eager than ever to learn who the ghost of Hathaway House was. So she had to find out as much as she could about the house itself. Most of all, she needed to study the history of the Hathaway family, who had been the only ones to live in the house.

This house has gotten a grip on me, Sam thought, as she examined the books in the study. *But I'm not sure if the grip is a warm hug or a stranglehold.*

Sam sat down with a book about New Hampshire history. It had a few paragraphs about Josiah Hathaway. His father had been an American officer in the Revolutionary War. Sam read that one of the Revolution's battles had been fought in the area around Endicott.

As a shipmaster-merchant, Josiah had owned about a dozen ships. He didn't travel on the ships himself, but he hired captains and crews who sailed the ships all over the world. The ships went from one foreign port to another, picking up all sorts of cargo. They went to exotic places like China; Sumatra and Java, in the East Indies; the Azores, off the west coast of Africa; and the West Indies. There they collected such valuable and desired items as coffee, sugar, rum, fruit, exotic spices, silks, elephant ivory, and porcelain objects. When the ships returned to Endicott, Josiah Hathaway sold the imported goods for very handsome prices.

Sam looked at the portrait of Josiah Hathaway that hung over the desk. Time had darkened the oil paint and caused spider-web cracks to run through it. Yet Josiah's eyes still gleamed, as blue as the bay—and just the hint of a smile continued to linger on the man's lips.

Could old Josiah be the ghost? Sam wondered. *Even if he's not, he must have some little secret that he's hiding behind his smile.*

Joe poked his head into the study. "David and I are taking Wishbone for a walk along the bay. Do you want to come?"

"No, thanks," Sam replied. "I'm going to hang around here. I'll see you all later."

Sam found no more books with helpful information. She began to walk around the house, studying every single one of the portraits. Each had a little plaque that gave the name of the person in the portrait and the date when it had been painted. Josiah Hathaway's portrait was the oldest, and the most recent portrait had been painted in 1924.

Aside from Josiah Hathaway, the only other name familiar to Sam was that of Hope Hathaway. She was the lady the lobster fishermen said had been murdered in the house. She was a delicate-looking woman, probably in her early twenties. Her portrait hung in one of the unused upstairs bedrooms.

There was one portrait Sam had come to like very much. It hung in the parlor, near the fireplace. Most of the portraits were square, but this one was oval. It featured a woman who looked to be in her forties. She wore a dress of shiny, green satin, against which she held a decorated fan. Even though she was made only of oil paint, her face seemed to radiate with beauty and warmth. The name on the plaque was "Lydia Hathaway."

"Find anything?"

Sam jumped, startled to see Wanda suddenly standing behind her. "Oh, Miss Gilmore, it's just you. I'm taking Miss Bridgewater's suggestion and doing some research on the Hathaway family."

"I wish I knew more about the Hathaways myself," Wanda said, rubbing her chin. "I know a lot more about the history of the Gilmores, my father's side of the family. Maybe you could check out that bookshop we saw in town. If it's open today, you might find some good historical information there."

"That's a great idea," Sam said. "Would you like to go with me?"

"I don't think so," Wanda said. "I want to spend some time examining all this wonderful old furniture in the house. And, Sam, take one of those umbrellas in the entrance hall. It's supposed to rain today."

"I'll do that," Sam said, as she ran up the stairs to get her jacket and camera.

Chapter Fifteen

Sam snapped a close-up photograph of a leaf drifting to the ground. Then she took a wider shot, capturing a group of trees that seemed to burn and blaze with their dazzling autumn colors. The scene was so beautiful, it could have been the perfect shot for a postcard. Sam was really looking forward to developing the roll of film. She was taking some spectacular photographs of the autumn scenery in New England.

Sam continued walking the short distance to the business district of Endicott. She passed a charming white church, which was built in the clapboard style. A few people were walking out after services, dressed up in their Sunday clothes. A group of young children broke away from the adults and began playing tag. The church, too, looked like a scene from a postcard. The peacefulness of the picture, however, was threatened by a dark storm cloud that hung directly over the church's bell tower.

Sam continued into the business area. She finally came to a bookshop on Front Street, right near the bay.

The name of the shop was Reading by the Sea. A sign on the door read:

MON.–FRI.: 10–5
SAT.: 12–5
SUNDAYS: ONLY SOMETIMES

A cardboard skeleton dangled above the sign, obviously a Halloween decoration.

Seeing a man inside, Sam realized this was one of those lucky Sundays when the bookshop was open. Sam entered the shop. It was a single room, in which books were arranged in an orderly way. Some of the books were new, but many of them seemed to be used.

A neatly dressed man who looked to be somewhere in his thirties sat at a desk. Wire-rimmed glasses made him seem like a professor.

"How may I help you?" the man said politely.

"A friend of mine just inherited Hathaway House," Sam explained. "I'm staying in the house with her for a few days, and I'm interested in learning whatever I can about the history of the Hathaway family."

"You haven't seen any ghosts in the house, have you?" the man said humorously.

"No . . . not really."

"I didn't think so. They say that house has been haunted for, oh, at least eighty years, but I'm not much of a believer in ghosts myself. Unfortunately, I don't have any books that give much information about the Hathaway family. However, I know a good bit about the town's history myself. Maybe I can be of help."

Sam didn't feel like explaining to the man that, yes,

the house was haunted after all. She was not certain how he would react.

"Well, do you know any really interesting stories about the Hathaway family?" Sam asked. "You know, dark secrets—that kind of thing."

The man thought for a moment. "There's been a rumor for a long time that a lady named Hope Hathaway was murdered in the house, but there's not a speck of evidence proving it's true. There's also a rumor about the man who built the house, Josiah Hathaway."

"Really? What's that?"

The bookshop man seemed to have a deep interest in the local history. "Back in the 1800s, the shipping merchants had to pay a large tax on every single item they imported into this country. As you probably know, Josiah Hathaway was a shipping merchant. Well, the authorities always suspected that Josiah was somehow cheating the government out of some of its tax money."

"So . . . he might have lied about how much he actually imported?"

"Well, it wasn't quite that simple. Let me show you."

The bookshop man led Sam outside and took her to the end of the block. From there, Sam had a clear view of the bay. She saw all the docks, boats, warehouses, and homes clustered around the tip of the bay's horseshoe shape. Black clouds were drifting over the water, like a fleet of airborne sailing ships.

About a mile down the rocky shore, the bay curved outward, blocking a piece of the shoreline from view. Right at that spot, Sam saw Hathaway House, which stood proudly on its hill of yellow-brown grass.

"Back in Josiah's day," the bookshop man said,

pointing, "there used to be a building right at the end of the bay. It was called the Customs House, and the men who worked there were the customs inspectors."

"Were they the ones in charge of figuring out how much tax to charge the shipowners?" Sam asked.

"Yes, they were. As soon as a ship docked in the bay, the customs inspectors would come aboard and search through the ship very carefully. Every single crate, barrel, and bale that had been imported from a foreign country was examined. Then a tax was figured out. Some of the goods were taxed by value, size, and others by weight."

"Then how could Josiah Hathaway have cheated? Could his ships have made a stop right by his house and unloaded some of their cargo there?"

The bookshop man chuckled. "Nice idea, but not possible. As you can see, the inspectors had a clear view of Hathaway House. If Josiah's men had been hauling cargo up that hill to the house, the inspectors would have seen it. Let me point out that Josiah Hathaway may *not* have been cheating. It's only a rumor. But, if he *was* cheating, the way he did it remains a mystery. Even to me."

Though Sam found this information interesting, she didn't see how this secret would make Josiah Hathaway a likely ghost suspect. But this was exactly the kind of detailed information Sam was searching for.

"Do you know any other interesting stories about the Hathaway family? I really want to learn as much as I possibly can."

"You're in luck then," the man said with a friendly smile. "I've got the leading authority on local history stashed away in the basement of my shop."

"Who's that?" Sam asked.

"*The Endicott Crier,*" the man replied. "It's our local newspaper. It's been published twice a week for a long time, and I've got copies of every single edition. There's no room for them at the newspaper office, so I keep them in my basement. Those papers should have plenty of information on the Hathaway family. You're welcome to have yourself a look."

"That would be great!" Sam said excitedly.

The man led Sam back into the shop, down a flight of steps, and into a tidy basement room. The walls were lined with shelves, and each shelf was stacked neatly with newspapers. Labels with dates were attached to the shelves.

"Unfortunately, there's no computerized system for locating articles on a particular subject," the bookshop man explained. "You'll just have to go through the

newspapers one by one. Have fun, put everything back in its proper place when you're done, and I'll be upstairs if you need anything."

"Thanks," Sam said, as the man headed upstairs.

The earliest newspapers in the room were from 1844. Sam pulled a stack of them down and set them on a table in the middle of the room. The newspapers were yellowed with age, brittle, partly torn, and the print looked odd. Even so, they were very readable. Sam began leafing through the newspapers, each of which was only a few pages.

After an hour, Sam had made her way to 1858. She had found various mentions of Josiah Hathaway and his immediate family, all of whom lived with him in Hathaway House. Sam discovered that Josiah Hathaway died peacefully at the ripe old age of seventy-seven.

A peaceful death was nice for him, but it doesn't help me too much, Sam thought, opening yet another newspaper. *According to Miss Bridgewater, people who die peacefully aren't as likely to turn into ghosts.*

Sam read on. As the years passed by, the newspapers became less yellowed and torn.

After Josiah's death, his eldest son, Isaac, became the master of Hathaway House. Soon after that, Josiah's other son, Zeke, was killed in the Civil War. Sam felt very bad for Zeke, but she somehow doubted that he was the ghost, because he had died in Pennsylvania.

Sam discovered that Hope Hathaway was the daughter of Isaac. Though Sam found several mentions of Hope, she read nothing to make her think that Hope Hathaway had been murdered. The paper reported that she had died of heart failure in 1871. She had been only twenty-three.

Poor Hope. I guess that death from heart failure isn't so peaceful. Even if she wasn't murdered, she could still be in the running for being the ghost.

Earlier in the day, Sam had seen portraits of all of the people she was reading about. As she read, she connected their faces with their stories. Doing this helped to make her research more fascinating. Sam got so hungry that she decided to take a quick break for lunch at a nearby sandwich shop. But she returned soon to the bookshop and its treasure of old newspapers.

Shortly after Hope Hathaway's death, her father, Isaac, died, peacefully. The next owner of the house was Marcus Hathaway, who had been a respected doctor in town. Lydia Hathaway, the lady in the portrait Sam liked so much, was his wife. They had taken over onwership of the house in 1876.

With great interest, Sam read a number of articles about Lydia Hathaway. Lydia had been the town's leading hostess, always entertaining guests in the house. Sometimes she gave large parties, to which most of the townsfolk were invited. Other times she had small groups of people over for such events as poetry readings and musical recitals. In addition, Lydia was very generous to people who had fallen on hard times. She often fed them and even allowed them to stay for a while in the upstairs rooms.

Sam was pleased to learn that Lydia Hathaway's personality was every bit as attractive as her portrait.

After reading about Lydia's peaceful death from old age in 1921, Sam ended her research. She remembered the bookshop man telling her that the house had been rumored to be haunted for at least eighty years. This meant there wasn't much chance it was the ghost of someone who had lived after the time of Lydia's death.

Sam had already done more than four hours of research. Her eyes weary, she put the last of the newspapers back in their proper place. Sam had learned so many inside details about the Hathaways that she almost felt as if she were a member of the family. But she still hadn't stumbled upon an easy answer to her biggest question: Who was the ghost?

Standing in the basement room, surrounded by thousands of newspapers, Sam closed her eyes. She allowed the portraits to float through her mind, as if they were characters in a movie.

Which one of you is still hanging around in this world?

Chapter Sixteen

Yikes! Wishbone thought with absolute horror. *The graveyard!*

Wishbone had just gone chasing after a football that Joe had thrown way over David's head. The ball had rolled a long way over the dead grass until it came to a stop right beside a black-iron fence. The fence surrounded the graveyard that lay just within eyesight of Hathaway House.

"Okay, I found the ball!" Wishbone called as David ran over. "Be really careful, though. The ball is right next to this—"

"Hey, Joe!" David called out. "Let's check out this graveyard! It might be kind of interesting!"

"Do you think it's all right?" Joe called as he jogged over.

"Sure," David said with a shrug. "Why not?"

"Why not?" Wishbone exclaimed. "Why not?! Because it's a graveyard—that's why not! I beg you boys not to go into that—"

David opened an unlocked gate. Then he and Joe stepped into the graveyard.

Why is it that no one ever listens to the dog?

Feeling responsible for his friends, Wishbone had no choice but to follow Joe and David onto the graveyard grounds. The dog passed through the open gateway, feeling uneasy.

About a hundred tombstones rose from the ground. Most of them were rectangular slabs of gray stone with rounded tops. They were all very simple, and most of them seemed to be rather old.

Wandering through any graveyard could be a creepy experience. To make things even spookier, it was twilight. The sun had been in and out from behind clouds all day. Just now it glowed low on the western horizon, and weird tints of red, gold, and orange shot through the sky. The angle of the sun made each tombstone cast a very long shadow.

To make the scene even more spooky, a low rumble of thunder announced an approaching storm. Wishbone's weather sense told him it would be a whopper.

The spookiest part of all was that it was Halloween!

Wishbone watched Joe and David walk among the tombstones. Wishbone knew that both boys had begun to believe in ghosts in the past twenty-four hours. The dog figured that might have had something to do with the boys' sudden interest in checking out the graves.

Myself, I like to bury things more than anyone I know. But I've never really had the itch to dig around in a graveyard.

"Aren't ghosts supposed to rise up from their resting places on Halloween?" Joe asked, crouching down to look at a tombstone.

"According to ancient tradition," David said, speaking in a quiet voice, "Halloween is the time when the spirits of all those who have died in the past year walk the Earth. Some people say it's also the night when evil spirits are the most likely to appear."

Wishbone felt the fur on his tail bristling.

"I believed all that stuff when I was younger," Joe said. "Then I realized it was all nonsense. But now I'm not so sure it is."

"I'm not so sure, either," David told his friend.

Suddenly, Wishbone sensed something nearby. He turned to see a sight so terrifying that it made every fur on his body bristle with fright.

The dog saw three figures walking along the dirt road not far off. One figure wore blood-red clothing from head to toe, and it carried a pitchfork. Another figure wore a flowing black gown and a triangular-shaped black hat. The third figure was covered with dark fur, even though it walked on two feet.

I know what those three are, Wishbone thought. *A devil, a witch, and a werewolf!*

"Watch out!" Wishbone yelled to his friends. "The monsters are coming! The monsters are coming! We've got to get ourselves out of sight! No time to waste!"

Wishbone began digging frantically at the ground. He hoped he could dig a hole deep enough for Joe, David, and himself to hide in.

Ugggh!!!

Suddenly, Wishbone stopped moving his paws. The dog realized that he was digging into ground where dead people were buried.

"Come on!" Wishbone insisted, seeing that Joe and

David still hadn't noticed the monsters. "We need to run for cover! Follow me!"

Wishbone ran behind the nearest object he could find. It was tall enough to hide his own body from view, but he wasn't sure it would be large enough to hide Joe and David.

Ahhhh!!!

Wishbone realized that he was hiding behind a tombstone.

The dog saw that Joe and David still hadn't noticed the creatures that were walking down the road. Weaving in and out of the tombstones, Wishbone made his way to David and Joe.

"Wishbone," Joe said, kneeling down to the dog. "What's gotten into you?"

"I'll tell you what's gotten into me! Look right over there, my friends! No, don't look over there! It might scare you too much! But if you did look over there, you'd see a devil, a witch, and a werewolf!"

David looked in the direction Wishbone had warned him not to look in. "I think he might be scared by those trick-or-treaters coming down the road."

"No! I'm not talking about the trick-or-treaters!" Wishbone insisted. "I'm talking about—"

Wishbone quickly took another look at the approaching devil, the witch, and the werewolf. This time, he realized that they were just little kids dressed in Halloween costumes. Judging by their height, they couldn't have been more than seven years old. Then Wishbone spotted a lady in regular clothing who was walking a little ways behind the kids. The terrier figured she was probably the mother of at least one of the "monsters."

Wishbone felt more embarrassed than he could ever remember feeling. However, he decided not to show it.

"Aw, shucks," Wishbone said with a chuckle. "I was trying to scare you guys into believing that those little kids were really a devil, a witch, and a werewolf. But I see that my little Halloween prank didn't work. Oh, well, can't win 'em all. How about if each of you gives me a treat, anyway?"

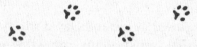

On her way back to Hathaway House, Sam was surprised to see Joe, David, and Wishbone standing in the graveyard.

As Sam came close to the fence, she called, "I've bumped into you guys in a lot of places. But this might be the strangest."

"It's pretty cool," David said, waving Sam over. "Come on in."

Sam stepped through the iron gateway and entered the graveyard. Bathed in the fading light, the graveyard seemed both gloomy and strangely beautiful. As Sam felt the wind blowing through her hair, she saw a leaf go skipping merrily past the graves.

"Here's the Hathaway family," Joe said, moving to another row of tombstones. "They all seem to be buried in this one area."

"Did you find anything interesting at the bookshop?" David asked Sam.

"Yes, I did," Sam said, walking over to the Hathaway graves. "I'll tell you about it just as soon as I take a look at some of these stones."

The first tombstone in the row looked ancient. The words etched into the stone were almost completely worn away by the weather and the passing of time. Sam could just barely make out the name: "Josiah Hathaway."

Sam went down the row, looking at each of the tombstones. She recognized the names of all the Hathaways she had seen on the portraits and read about in the newspapers. The approaching darkness seemed to change the gray slabs of stone into living shadows.

Finally, Sam found the grave that interested her the most. A rose was carved into the upper part of the stone. Below, an inscription read:

IN MEMORY OF LYDIA HATHAWAY,
WHO DIED IN 1921 IN
THE SEVENTY-FIFTH YEAR OF HER AGE.
SHE WELCOMED EVERYONE INTO HER HOME.

I wonder if Lydia Hathaway could be the ghost, Sam thought, kneeling down to the tombstone. *If the haunting started about eighty years ago, that would have been just around the time of her death. But she doesn't seem like the ghost type to me. She lived such a long and full life.*

Sam thought about Miss Bridgewater's four *r's.*

Lydia died peacefully, so I doubt that she had a strong need for resolve. She seems far too nice to be out for revenge or to be angry at somebody for renovating Hathaway House. Refusal, hmm . . . She might have liked life so much that she refuses to leave it. But, even so, somehow that doesn't sound like her.

Sam thought about the different qualities of the ghost in Hathaway House. It gave off a lavender scent, it made a teakettle whistle, and it liked the wind chimes and the music box. Sam was beginning to wonder if there might be more than one ghost in the house. Miss Bridgewater had mentioned that as a possibility.

Sam glanced around at all the neighboring graves. Then she looked toward the gray shape of Hathaway House, which stood just a short distance away.

Once more Sam looked at Lydia's tombstone. She took special notice of the words "She welcomed everyone into her Home."

Hmm . . . I'm starting to think of a very interesting theory. Maybe Lydia Hathaway isn't actually the ghost. But she was such a good-hearted hostess, maybe she filled the house with a spirit of welcomeness. Maybe some of the people in this very graveyard have a refusal problem. For one reason or another, they just aren't ready yet to let go of this world. And maybe, because of Lydia's welcoming spirit, they feel welcome to hang out in Hathaway House.

Sam knew it was an incredible theory, but everything else that had already happened in Endicott had been incredible. At this point, Sam felt her theory almost made perfect sense.

That's who I think the ghosts are! Sam thought with triumph. *Visitors from the graveyard! I have to find out if I'm right! I just have to!*

Cold raindrops began pelting Sam's face.

"Here comes the rain," Joe called, as he, David, and Wishbone began racing toward Hathaway House. "Let's get out of here!"

Sam wasn't in quite as big of a hurry because she had an umbrella. She opened it up, gave a farewell wave to Lydia's tombstone, then walked slowly out of the graveyard. The raindrops drummed against the umbrella like the patter of running footsteps.

Sam saw three kids in Halloween costumes walking hurriedly down the road nearby. They looked to be around seven years old. The rain had made them put an end to their trick-or-treating adventure. A woman was standing in the middle of the group, protecting the kids with a large umbrella.

Sam stopped to watch the kids, who looked so cute. They were dressed as a devil, a witch, and a werewolf. Sam heard the devil complain loudly about the sudden rain.

It seemed to Sam that only yesterday she had been going from door to door in Oakdale, gathering Halloween candy. Sam remembered some of the great costumes she had worn. Her favorite was the evil-princess costume, complete with a crown and clawlike fingernails. She had scared herself just by looking in the mirror.

Well, my Halloween days of trick-or-treating are over,

Sam thought with sadness. *Maybe that's why I've become so interested in the haunting of Hathaway House. A ghost is a dead person who isn't quite ready to leave its life yet. It's kind of like the way I feel about my childhood. It seems as if it's nearing an end, and yet . . . I'm not quite ready to let go of it.*

As the rain fell harder, Sam picked up her pace and walked quickly over to Hathaway House. When she stepped into the hallway, she wiped her shoes on a doormat and set down the umbrella.

"Welcome back," Wanda said, as she met the girl in the entrance hall. "Joe, David, and Wishbone are upstairs drying off."

"Did any trick-or-treaters come by here?" Sam asked, noticing a bowl of candy by the front door.

"Just a few," Wanda said. "It was a good thing I picked up some candy at that candy shop yesterday. But I'm afraid this rain will put an early end to the night's trick-or-treating. I heard on the radio that a big storm is coming. Flooding is even expected around here. It's a shame for the kids."

"Miss Gilmore," Sam said, as she wiped away some water with a towel, "could we have a séance tonight?"

Wanda shook her head. "Sam, I don't think that's a good idea."

"Miss Bridgewater made the suggestion herself."

"Yes, but Miss Bridgewater is not the one responsible for you kids. I am. It's bad enough that we're staying in a haunted house. I think having a séance would just be pushing things too far."

"Please," Sam pleaded.

Wanda looked at Sam curiously. "Sam, why is this séance so important to you?"

Sam told Wanda her theory about the ghosts being visitors from the graveyard. She also confided in Wanda about feeling sad that her childhood was quickly slipping away.

Wanda listened very carefully, a look of understanding in her eyes. When Sam was through talking, Wanda said, "Well, all right. Let's have ourselves a séance tonight."

"Oh, thank you so much!" Sam cried happily.

"I just hope I don't regret this," Wanda said with a sigh.

Chapter Seventeen

The séance began shortly after the grandfather clock sounded its eight o'clock gongs.

Wishbone heard the rain beating away at the house, as it had been doing for the past few hours. The rain was pouring down so fast and furious that the dog hoped it wouldn't tear the old house apart.

Joe, Sam, David, and Wanda sat on the parlor floor, gathered around the coffee table. They were holding hands, each acting very serious. They had turned all the lights out, and they had lit all the candles in the room. Through the darkness, the candle flames glimmered and glowed, like tiny living creatures.

Wishbone decided not to join the hand-holding. First, he didn't have hands, and, second, he got restless if someone held his paws for too long. Instead, the dog seated himself right beside the coffee table.

The study contained several books on the subject of ghosts. Before dinner, David had flipped through the books, looking for information on séances. He would be the séance's advisor. It was agreed that Wanda would be the medium, because of the previous experience she had with the job.

Just before the séance began, the group had gone through the house, checking to make sure that no one had recently sneaked into the place. David had called this "experiment control."

"Now what do we do?" Sam asked.

"We should all concentrate on welcoming the ghost into our presence," David explained. "I guess we should just think friendly thoughts. We're holding hands in order to allow our thoughts to merge together into one bigger thought."

"Do you think we have enough psychic power to pull this off?" Joe asked.

"We might," David replied. "One of the books I looked at says that the more the ghost wants to make itself known, the less it matters about the actual power of the medium and the other participants. It seems that our ghost isn't very shy."

"Do we close our eyes?" Sam asked.

"Yes," David said. "The book said it might help us concentrate better."

"No peeking, anyone," Wishbone warned.

The dog shut his eyes tight. Everything turned to blackness.

Wishbone smelled scents of excited nervousness coming from all his friends. He felt the same way himself.

"Miss Gilmore, invite the ghost to join us," Wishbone heard David say.

After clearing her throat, Wanda spoke. "Ghostly spirit, my name is Wanda Gilmore. I may soon become

the new owner of this house, so I would very much like to meet you. I'm here with some very good friends of mine. There's Joe, Sam, David, and . . . uh . . . the furry fellow is Wishbone."

I wish she would stop introducing me that way! Wishbone thought with annoyance.

"If you are in this house, please show us a sign that you are here," Wanda continued. "Any sign will do. But I would prefer it if you didn't break anything."

Joe let out a chuckle.

"Shh!" Sam urged.

Everyone waited in silence. Several long, dark, silent moments crept by.

Eyes kept shut, Wishbone smelled all the old scents of Hathaway House and all the familiar scents coming from his friends. He grew a little hungry as he also smelled the leftover aromas from the evening's fish-and-spinach dinner.

A new scent began mingling with the others. It was the sweet-springlike-flowery scent of lavender. That was the very same scent that had been given off by the ghost that had appeared in the parlor the previous night.

"Hey, guys," Wishbone whispered. "I'm picking up a ghostly signal here."

No one said anything in reply.

Wishbone began picking up another scent, although the new one was much fainter than the lavender. It was the Bay Rum cologne, the same scent Wishbone had smelled in Joe's bedroom Friday night.

Several moments later, Sam exclaimed, "I smell the lavender! The ghost must be here! The same one from last night!"

"I smell it, too," Joe said with amazement. "Have we really made contact with a ghost?"

"Oh, my gosh! This is so exciting!" Wanda said, barely able to control herself. "I've summoned a ghost! We've summoned a ghost! Well, *someone* has summoned a ghost!"

"We need to keep concentrating and keep our eyes closed," David said, doing his best to sound calm. "If we let our concentration fade, the ghost may slip away. Miss Gilmore, try asking the ghost some questions."

"Remember," Sam whispered, "we're trying to find out who the ghost is and what it wants."

Wanda spoke in a very serious voice. "Ghostly spirit, I . . . uh . . . would like to ask you a few questions, if you don't mind. If the answer is 'yes,' give one tap of some kind. If the answer is 'no,' give two taps. Feel free to tap on anything you can get your hands on—if you have hands. Do you understand?"

Several moments passed.

A single knock was heard.

The knock sounded to Wishbone like knuckles rapping on a wooden surface. Wishbone was eager to open his eyes, but he knew that might break the chain of concentration. Besides, he knew the ghost would probably be invisible, as it had been the previous night.

"The ghost understands us," David whispered.

"Try to find out who it is," Sam whispered.

"Are you a woman?" Wanda asked the ghost.

A single knock was heard.

That would be a "yes," Wishbone thought.

"Are you younger than twenty-five?" Wanda asked.

A single knock sounded.

Another "yes." Why do I feel as if we're all appearing on a game show?

"Are you Hope Hathaway?" Wanda asked.

Two knocks sounded.

Oh, so it's not Hope Hathaway. That means those fishy lobster fishermen were wrong.

"Are you a member of the Hathaway family?" Wanda asked.

Two knocks sounded.

"Ah, she's not a Hathaway," Joe whispered. "That's interesting."

"Ask if there is more than one ghost," Sam whispered.

"Are you the only ghost in this house?" Wanda asked.

Two knocks sounded.

Aha! That means there's more than one ghost lurking around in this joint. Boy, Wanda really knows how to pick her property.

"Do you know the other ghosts in the house?" Wanda asked.

A single knock sounded, meaning "yes."

"Do you mind if I share the house with you?" Wanda asked.

Two knocks sounded, meaning "no."

"Does anyone have any questions?" Wanda whispered to her friends.

"Ask if we can meet some of the other ghosts," Sam whispered.

"We would very much like to meet some of the other ghosts," Wanda told the spirit. "I think it would be a good idea, since I might be living in this house for part of the year. Don't you?"

A single knock sounded, meaning "yes."

Eyes still shut, Wishbone raised his ears high. If more ghosts were coming, he wanted to be the first to know about it. He realized that all the scents of nervousness were gone. He and his friends had become relaxed with the séance.

Soon Wishbone heard tubes of metal clinking back and forth against one another. They made a pleasantly musical sound.

"That sounds like the wind chimes in my room," Sam whispered with excitement. "That must be the ghost who visited me up there."

The music of the wind chimes faded. Wishbone's ears twitched as he heard a screechy-dragging-clicking noise. For some reason, the noise reminded Wishbone of a classroom.

"It's chalk scratching on a blackboard," said David.

Wheeeeeeee!!!

Immediately, Wishbone lowered his ears. He recognized the sound all too well as the shriek of a teakettle.

"That must be the ghost who keeps boiling our water," Sam called over the whistling noise.

As the whistle faded, Wishbone heard the hollow-rubbery-tapping noise, which he recognized as the bouncing ball.

"That's the ball I heard bouncing the other night," Wishbone told his friends.

"What is that?" Wanda asked with confusion.

"I just told you what it is!" Wishbone exclaimed. "A bouncing ball!"

"It sounds like a ball bouncing," Joe whispered.

I wonder if the ghosts can understand me better than the humans can.

186

The sound of the bouncing ball was replaced by another noise familiar to Wishbone. It was a series of high-pitched squeaks. Wishbone recognized the squeaks as the sound he made whenever he bit into one of his rubber squeaky toys.

"It sounds like one of Wishbone's squeaky toys," Joe said with surprise.

"Maybe it's the ghost of a dog," Wanda whispered.

Wishbone's tail came to life, wagging with happiness. "Hey, Ghost Dog! Can you hear me? My name is Wishbone! I'm a dog, too! A very handsome Jack Russell terrier! I'm so glad to meet you, pal! What's it like over on your side of the fence? Hey, tell me something—when you become a haunted hound, what sort of food do you have served to you?"

Sam's eyes were shut, but the rest of her senses were wide open with wonder.

It pleased her to discover that she had been right about there being more than one ghost in the house. At the moment, there seemed to be six ghostly guests. In her mind, Sam assigned them different personalities. The "lavender" ghost was a young woman. The "wind chimes" ghost was a dedicated musician. The "blackboard" ghost was a strict schoolteacher. The "teakettle" ghost was an energetic cook. The "bouncing ball" ghost was a mischievous young boy. The "squeaky toy" ghost was a fun-loving dog.

As if answering "yes" to Sam's guesses, the ghostly noises began joining together. They sounded all at once, filling the room with a joyful chorus of otherworldly noise. All the while, the lavender scent floated through the room, as if that ghost were the conductor.

The house feels as if it's filled with so much life, Sam thought, her heart beating rapidly with excitement. *It's as if I'm attending a party. The wildest, weirdest, most wonderful Halloween party ever given! I ought to be scared out of my wits. But, strangely enough, I'm not. For some reason, I'm incredibly happy.*

Sam could sense that her friends were also enjoying the experience.

"Are you having fun!" Wanda called out to the ghosts.

Over the noise, a single knock sounded, the ghost answer for "yes."

"I'm glad you're having fun," Wanda said cheerfully. "Because I'm having fun, too. I wasn't sure I liked having ghosts in the house, but you folks are rather charming. I'll tell you this right now. If I keep this house, all of you ghosts will be welcome here anytime you like!"

One after another, the noises began fading away into silence. Even the strong scent of lavender seemed to be disappearing.

"They're leaving," Joe whispered in a tone of disappointment.

"Are there any more questions I should ask before they're gone?" Wanda whispered.

"Ask the lavender lady why she feels so welcome in Hathaway House," Sam whispered.

"Oh, Miss Lavender Ghost!" Wanda called out. "Why do you feel so welcome in Hathaway House?"

"You can't ask it that way, Miss Gilmore," Joe whispered. "Remember, it has to be a 'yes' or 'no' question."

"Maybe not," David whispered. "The book said ghosts can give signs that answer questions."

"Could you please show me a sign that indicates why you folks feel so welcome in the house?" Wanda called out.

There was only the sound of a fierce rainfall, and the smell of a fading scent of lavender.

Sam really wanted an answer to this question, and she realized the sign might be a visual one.

She opened her eyes and sneaked a peek.

The parlor was a blur of darkness, broken only by tiny flickers from the many candles. Sam looked around, searching for anything unusual. Finally, her eyes fell on the oval portrait of Lydia Hathaway.

The portrait was tilting!

I'm right! The ghosts are here because of Lydia Hathaway! I just knew that was the reason!

The next second, Sam saw something else, right beneath the portrait. She saw two moving shapes. They seemed to be . . .

A pair of human hands!

A startled sound flew out of Sam's mouth.

"What is it?" Joe asked, his eyes shooting open.

The sight of the hands was the most frightening thing yet. Sam was so terrified she couldn't speak a word.

All around the table, eyes opened and linked hands dropped. David rushed to switch on a lamp, which added brighter light to the room.

Wanda hurried over to Sam, kneeling beside her. "Sam, are you all right?"

Still unable to speak, Sam forced herself to nod.

"Breathe deeply," Wanda said, putting an arm

around Sam. "Come on, now. In and out. In and out. Deep breaths."

Sam forced herself to take in a deep breath, then let it out. She repeated the pattern a few times.

"Tell us what happened," Wanda urged.

"I opened my eyes," Sam managed to say. "And I . . . saw . . . a pair of *real* hands."

"Where?" David asked.

Sam pointed to the spot, but the hands were no longer there. "They were coming through the wall. Right beneath the portrait of Lydia Hathaway. See? The portrait is tilted to one side just a little bit. That was done by living human hands!"

David and Joe switched on more lamps, then went over to the portrait. They both ran their hands and eyes over the wood paneling on the wall. Wishbone went over and pawed at the floor, as if he wanted to help with the investigation.

"There doesn't seem to be any secret opening," David said, eyeing the wall very carefully. "There's no crack or moving parts."

"I don't see anything, either," Joe said, feeling the wall with his fingers. "I really don't see how a pair of hands could come through here. Are you sure this is the right spot, Sam?"

"I'm positive," Sam answered.

Wanda kept an arm around Sam. "It was very dark in here, Sam. Is it possible you imagined the hands? After all, this whole experience has been pretty unusual."

"No, I'm *sure* that I saw the hands," Sam replied. "At least . . . I'm pretty sure of it. I guess that maybe the portrait could already have been tilted, but . . . no, I really think I saw a pair of hands!"

Wanda, Joe, and David each nodded with understanding.

David switched on a few more lamps, making the room as bright as possible. Wishbone nestled his body against Sam, trying to give her comfort.

"Sam, I know this is a strange question," David said. "But could those have been ghostly hands?"

"I really don't think so," Sam replied. "I'm pretty sure they were just a regular pair of living human hands."

"If they were," Wanda said grimly, "that means someone is inside the house with us. A living, breathing, human being. Maybe a dangerous person."

Joe looked around. "Maybe this person has been inside Hathaway House a lot lately. But how is this person getting in? The tape is always in place at all of the doors and windows, we've checked every single possible hiding spot, and there's no sign at all of a secret passageway that leads into the house."

"The hands also mean something else," David said, rubbing his lower lip. "They mean that all of the ghostly stuff we've seen has probably been fake. I don't see how this person could have done it, but . . ."

"I think I preferred being scared by a ghost rather than a real person," Sam said.

Wanda sprang to her feet. "Okay, this does it. I am responsible for you kids, and I am not taking any more chances. Everyone go pack your things. We are leaving Hathaway House!"

"I don't know if we should risk leaving in this weather," Joe said, glancing at a rain-lashed window. "The roads around here could very well be flooded. Besides, I don't think there are any motels nearby."

Sam heard the rain pounding at the house with tremendous power. Sam felt trapped, not to mention a bit sick to her stomach.

"Oh, I just don't know what we should do," Wanda said, pacing back and forth in the room like a caged animal. "Maybe I should call Teddy Lyman. He might have some advice for us."

"I don't like that idea," David said, shaking his head. "Don't forget, he's one of our suspects."

"Staying in the house might not be so bad," Joe said. "If Sam *did* see a pair of real human hands—"

"I *did!*" Sam insisted.

"Well," Joe continued, "they were probably the hands of the person—or persons—who is trying to make us think the house is haunted. It seems this person—or persons—is trying to scare us, not hurt us. I really think we'll be okay."

"Even so," Sam argued, "I don't like knowing that some stranger is inside the house with us."

"I don't like it, either," Joe agreed. "But I doubt that whoever it is will . . . well, I don't think anyone is going to hurt us."

Wanda knelt down, placing logs in the fireplace. "It's settled, then. For now, we'll just stay put in the house. I'll call the local police about a possible intruder. And listen to me. Tonight, we need to stick together at all times. No one goes anywhere alone!"

"I wouldn't dream of it," Sam said softly.

Chapter Eighteen

Like sardines in a can, Joe, Sam, and David sat crowded together on the parlor sofa. Wanda sat right beside them in the rocking chair. Wishbone lay nearby on the floor. The dog could smell a strong scent of fear coming from each of his friends.

A fire burned in the fireplace. A bowl of freshly popped popcorn sat on the coffee table.

The group was doing a very familiar and comforting activity—watching TV. They were watching an old black-and-white movie, a comedy. The old TV set showed as much static as picture, but no one complained.

Sam dropped a few pieces of popcorn for Wishbone.

"Thanks," Wishbone said, after gobbling the treat.

About a half hour earlier, Wanda had called the local police. A very nice officer had come to the house, asking questions and looking around. As he left, he promised he would respond within minutes if Wanda and the others needed him. This made everyone feel safer.

Wishbone kept his ears raised high, though, on high

alert for any sign that danger was near. The dog heard many sounds—rain hammering on the house, the loud tick of the grandfather clock, spoken dialogue from the movie. But he heard no intruder.

Time passed. . . .

The movie ended. The popcorn bowl was empty. The grandfather clock sounded its ten o'clock gongs.

The local news came on, and the storm was the lead story. The newscaster reported that many of the smaller roads had been flooded along the New Hampshire seacoast.

After the news ended, another movie came on. The group decided to watch it. No one was in the mood for sleep.

More time passed. . . .

The second movie ended. The grandfather clock sounded its midnight gongs. The rain had stopped, but the windows were still dripping with water. Joe, Sam, David, and Wanda headed for their upstairs rooms. Wishbone began following the group to the entrance hall.

Suddenly, Wishbone froze in his tracks.

A pair of greenish-yellow eyes were burning through the parlor window.

The black witch-cat is back! Wishbone thought with alarm. *Could a witch-cat make a pair of hands appear through the wall? Sure! Why not? There's no telling how strong the powers of a witch-cat can be. And there's no telling what this witch-cat might have in store for us next. Okay, no more playing around. I need to find out what this creature is up to, once and for all!*

Wishbone hurried into the kitchen, passed through the doggie door, and ran around to the front of the house.

The dead grass and crawling weeds were drenched with rainwater. All was silence and darkness. After the fury of the storm, the night had become eerily calm.

Wishbone looked around, hearing paws pattering over the soaked ground. He spotted the shadow-black cat disappearing into the night.

Here I go again, Wishbone thought, as he set off after the cat. *The cat will probably lead me back to the cat coven. I'll just have to deal with that. The safety of my friends is at stake here.*

The night was as black as a witch's hat, and every step turned Wishbone's paws muddier and wetter. But the dog kept his nose on the trail of the black cat's scent. He traveled along the dirt road, through the trees, past the houses, by the church, and, finally, into the alleyway behind The Portside Tavern.

Again, more than a dozen cats were gathered in a circle. Again, they were in the middle of some mysterious activity. By then, the black cat had taken its place among the coven.

His tail wagging nervously, Wishbone crept toward the cats. He was determined not to chicken out this time. He felt certain the cats were doing something incredibly awful, but he needed to know exactly *what* it was. Only then would he be sure of what he and his friends were up against.

As Wishbone neared the circle, every single cat turned to him. Countless feline eyes glowed through the darkness, as if sending out an evil spell. Several of the eyes reflected off the alley's rain-slickened concrete.

Digging deep to find every ounce of his courage, Wishbone made his way inside the circle. Surrounded by all the cats, he saw a sight that made his lower muzzle drop open with shock. He saw . . . garbage.

All sorts of garbage lay strewn on the ground—scraps of bread, opened tin cans, fish flesh clinging to bits of bone, broken pieces of lobster shell, peeled potato skins, and much more.

So that's what the cat activity is—eating garbage!

Wishbone glanced at the industrial-sized trash cans that stood by the restaurant's back door. Several stuffed plastic bags sat next to them. Wishbone could see that the cats had torn holes in the bags, through which they had taken their precious garbage-food.

Soon the cats returned to their feast, as if Wishbone wasn't even there. They clawed and pawed and picked and licked and chewed. One of the cats was already cleaning its fur with careful catlike attention to detail.

The truth is out, Wishbone thought with great relief. *These cats aren't witches. They're not even wicked. They're just really hungry. This means the cats definitely aren't the ones causing the trouble at Hathaway House.*

Wishbone looked at the black cat, which was digging into the scraps clinging to a lobster shell. Wishbone stared at the cat until it turned its greenish-yellow eyes on him. The black cat no longer seemed to look so . . . dangerous.

Suddenly, I feel like giving that black cat a good old fashioned chase. I'd better not, though. My first duty is to get back to ground zero and make sure all my friends stay safe and sound.

Wishbone trotted out of the alley, pleased with his detective work. He realized he could take a shortcut back to Hathaway House by following the shoreline of the bay. Soon he was racing along the wet sand, which was heavily peppered with pebbles. Waves broke against the rocky outcroppings that jutted into the water.

In less than ten minutes, Wishbone approached the hill where Hathaway House sat. A bare hint of moonlight peeked out from behind leftover storm clouds. The moon's glow fell on the house in such a way that it made the house's "face" seem to wear a slight smile.

A row of big rocks lined the bottom of the hill, as if they were phantom soldiers standing watch. Wishbone spent a few moments figuring out how we would get up and over the rocks. Suddenly, his nose picked up a familiar scent—Bay Rum cologne.

I've been smelling that a lot lately. I first smelled it when I heard the bouncing ball in Joe's bedroom. I also smelled it at the séance. I think I may have smelled it a few other times, too. At first, I thought it was a ghostly smell. But now it seems we're not dealing with a ghost, or a witch, or anything super-natural. So this might be a human smell. As a matter of fact, the Bay Rum might be coming from the person who is pretending to haunt Hathaway House!

Wishbone followed the scent of the Bay Rum, even though it was very faint in the open air. The dog's nose led him to one of the big rocks at the bottom of the hill.

The Bay Rum smell seems to be strongest right around this rock. In fact, it seems to be coming from behind this rock. But that doesn't make any sense unless . . . there's a secret passageway there.

Wishbone pawed at the rock. It didn't budge an inch. The dog tried digging a hole, but the rock seemed to extend far underground. Again the dog pawed at the big rock, but it stood firm as . . . a rock.

I need some more muscle to do this job.

"Joe, Sam, David, Wanda!" Wishbone called in his loudest voice. "I need you down here on the double! I've got something we need to investigate!"

The night remained silent.

Why don't they ever listen to me?

Wishbone thought about running up to the house to get his friends. But he didn't want to leave his post. There was a chance the bad guy would come in or out of the secret passageway any minute, and Wishbone wanted to be there if it happened.

Again Wishbone called up to the house. "Joe, Sam, David, Wanda! Come down here right away! I've picked up the scent of something very important!"

Chapter Nineteen

Joe turned over in bed and glanced at the neon numbers on the alarm clock. It was 12:47. Joe had been in bed for almost half an hour, but he hadn't even come close to falling asleep yet. Outside, rainwater gurgled through a metal gutter.

It had been decided that no one would stay alone. Joe was staying in David's room, and Sam was staying just down the hall in Wanda's room. Joe hadn't seen Wishbone for a while, and he figured the dog was staying with Sam and Wanda. Joe looked over at David, who was lying face-down on the room's other bed.

"David," Joe whispered, "are you asleep?"

"Not really," David mumbled. "I'm trying, though."

Even after munching on plenty of popcorn and watching two old movies on television, nobody had really managed to relax completely. There had not been another sign of danger so far, but the night was far from over. Morning seemed to be several years away.

Joe saw a black spider crawl up the wall. He thought

it incredible how the spider's thin legs could carry it up a sideways surface.

It was almost as incredible as the recent events in Hathaway House. First, it had seemed that the hauntings were caused by a prankster. Then a professional ghost investigator had *proved* the hauntings were real. Then Sam had seen a pair of real, live human hands come through a wall. If that were true, it meant the hauntings were probably fake, after all.

But if the hauntings were fake, how could the prankster have been getting into the house? Every possible hiding place and way of entering the house had been checked over and over again. And no one had found, or even heard of, a secret passageway leading to the house.

Even so, it seemed that some uninvited guest was spending time in the house. This someone could even be in the house right now. The someone might even be watching Joe watch the spider right this very second.

Joe felt the little hairs at the back of his neck bristle. He hadn't felt this afraid since . . . the days when he used to believe in ghosts.

Joe sat up in bed and reached for a set of handgrips that he used to strengthen his forearms. He wouldn't let fear get the best of him. He would stay awake all night, keeping his eyes and ears alert for anything sinister. Aside from his mother, Sam, David, Wanda, and Wishbone were his very best friends in the world. Joe would do everything in his power to make sure no harm came to any of them during the night.

Sam turned a page in *The House of the Seven Gables*. She was nearing the end of the book's final chapter.

Though she sat in a rocking chair, she tried not to rock so she wouldn't make any noise. A few feet away, Wanda was sleeping in the large bed with the green-tassled canopy. Sam doubted that Wanda was sleeping very well, because Wanda kept rolling around restlessly.

Did I really see a pair of human hands . . . or was I just imagining it? Sam wondered for the hundredth time. *I'm pretty sure I really saw them.*

To keep herself from running the question through her mind over and over again, Sam turned her attention back to her book.

In the story, Holgrave, the young daguerreotype artist, had come home to discover the dead body of Judge Pyncheon sitting in the parlor. Shortly after, Phoebe, Hepzibah, and Clifford had returned to the house. Hepzibah was still worried that Clifford might be accused of murdering the man.

However, Holgrave pointed out that the judge had not been murdered, nor had he died as a result of Matthew Maule's curse from many years ago—"God will give him blood to drink." It was obvious, Holgrave claimed, that both Judge Pyncheon and his ancestor Colonel Pyncheon died from a breathing disease known as apoplexy.

Hepzibah explained that Judge Pyncheon came to the house because he believed Clifford knew the whereabouts of some long-lost document. Indeed, Clifford had a blurry memory of such a document, but he couldn't remember where it was stashed away.

Surprisingly, Holgrave knew the answer. When he

pushed a secret button, the portrait of Colonel Pyncheon moved forward, then tumbled to the floor. A secret compartment was revealed in the wall. A dusty piece of paper laid there. It was a legal document that once belonged to Colonel Pyncheon. The document stated that the Pyncheon family had ownership of a vast amount of land in the state of Maine. Though the greedy Judge Pyncheon did not realize it, the document was now outdated and worthless.

Sam realized this was the secret of the portrait—the secret supposedly only the ghosts knew. But it turned out that a single living person, Holgrave, also knew the secret of the portrait.

Holgrave revealed that the carpenter who built the House of the Seven Gables was actually Matthew Maule's son. The carpenter built the hiding place, stole the document from Colonel Pyncheon, then hid the document. He did this to get revenge on the colonel, who had seen to it that Matthew Maule was hanged for practicing witchcraft. Holgrave knew about the hiding place because he was, in fact, an ancestor of Matthew Maule's. The hiding place was an age-old secret known only to members of the Maule family.

Holgrave, Phoebe, Hepzibah, and Clifford decided to move to a simple cottage in the country. Holgrave and Phoebe planned to be married. Hepzibah and Clifford would be able to live peacefully, free of their troubled past. The House of the Seven Gables would remain empty—except for its never-dying memories.

Memories are a lot like ghosts, Sam thought, as she closed her book. *I guess they have a way of making an old house feel haunted, even if it's not.*

Sam glanced at the nearby dresser. She realized it had stored clothing of many different fashions for many different people through many different time periods. As Sam looked across the room at the vanity table, she was startled to see a face. Then she realized it was only her own reflection in the speckled mirror.

Hathaway House has sheltered so many people and seen so many things, it seems to have taken on a life of its own. There must be memories in every corner, closet, and cobweb. And the house itself has secrets, too. I'm sure of that. In a way, it's too bad these walls can't talk.

Arrrrf!

Sam heard the faint sound of a dog barking, coming from outside. She had assumed Wishbone was with Joe and David, but the bark sounded very familiar.

Sam went to the bedroom's open three-sided window. Through the night's darkness, she saw the dim outline of the hill and the waters of the bay. Sam heard the very

faint bark again. It sounded as if it was coming from somewhere near the water.

"What is it?" Wanda mumbled, sitting up in bed, sensing something was wrong.

Before Sam could answer, Joe and David rushed into the room, both wearing sweats and T-shirts.

"Didn't that sound like Wishbone barking?" Joe asked anxiously.

"Yes, it did," Sam replied. "He seems to be right by the bay. But how could he have gotten outside?"

"There's the doggie door in the kitchen," David pointed out.

"He might be in trouble," Joe said, heading toward the door. "I'd better go find him."

"Not by yourself," Wanda said, climbing out of bed. "Tonight we stick together."

"Do we have a flashlight?" Sam asked.

"No, not yet," Joe said, looking very worried. "But I really need to get out there."

Wanda began pulling on a pair of pants over her pajama bottoms. "Okay, the three of you go and look for Wishbone down by the bay. I'll join you as soon as I get a flashlight."

Within minutes, Joe, Sam, and David had thrown on clothes and their jackets and had rushed out the front door. The kids hurried down the gentle slope of the hill. The night was completely dark, except for some lamplight that shone out of a few of Hathaway House's windows. Sam felt her shoes sloshing in leftover rainwater as she moved across the dirt, sand, and dead grass of the hillside.

Finally, the kids climbed over some rocks and

stepped onto the pebbly ground by the shore. They saw Wishbone standing by the rocks that lined the bottom of the hill.

The dog didn't seem to be hurt, but he moved around as if something was bothering him. He looked at the kids, then at the rocks, then gave a sharp bark.

"Something's bugging him," Joe said, kneeling down to the dog. "Maybe he smells a rat or a squirrel by the rocks."

"Are there squirrels around here?" David asked.

"Who knows?" Joe said with a shrug.

Sam wondered if Wishbone had stumbled on something of more importance than a stray animal. He often seemed to have an intelligence far beyond that of the average dog. For some reason, he was especially helpful when it came to solving a mysterious situation.

"Come on, let's get back up to the house," Joe said, lifting Wishbone into his arms.

"Yeah, let's head back," David agreed.

"No, wait," Sam said, holding up a hand. "Just let me think a minute."

Sam's mind wandered back to *The House of the Seven Gables*.

In the book, there was a secret compartment. But it was known only to the ghosts—and to Holgrave, who knew about it because he was an ancestor of Matthew Maule's. Maybe Hathaway House has a secret passageway known only to a Hathaway descendant.

Sam stared at Wishbone. *Could Wishbone have discovered something that might be part of a secret passageway to the house? No, there can't be a secret passageway. We've searched the house with a fine-tooth comb. Besides, if there was a secret passageway, it couldn't be that much of a secret anymore. Somebody would have mentioned it to us. Mr. Whipple or Mr. Lyman or that guy at the bookshop. Except . . .*

Sam remembered how she and her friends had wondered if some relative of Homer Hathaway's could have been jealous that Wanda was due to inherit the house. Maybe this relative knew of a secret passageway and was using it to scare the Oakdale visitors away.

But why would there be a secret passageway in the first place?

In her mind, Sam saw the hint of a smile on Josiah Hathaway's lips.

If there is a secret passageway, it may very well have something to do with Josiah Hathaway. I always thought he was hiding something. But where? . . .

Sam turned her eyes to the bay. The water was just a mass of blackness, every bit as dark as the night sky. The water washed against the rocks and pebbles of the shore. Sam glanced up the hill at the square shape of Hathaway House.

Of course! The secret passageway could be right here! This would be the perfect place for it!

"Sam, what's on your mind?" David asked.

"Remember what I told you about Josiah Hathaway?" Sam told David and Joe. "How he was suspected of sneaking some of his imported goods past the customs inspectors?"

"Sure, we remember," Joe said. "What about it?"

"From the business district, you can see Hathaway House," Sam explained. "But you can't see the shoreline right here in front of the house. That's because of the curve of the bay. Maybe Josiah Hathaway had his ships make a quick stop right here before they went into the harbor. Then the crew would quickly unload some of the cargo, unseen by anyone in town."

"But then what would the crew do with the cargo?" David asked. "If they carried it up the hill to the house, they would be seen."

"That's what I'm getting at," Sam said, reaching over to pet Wishbone. "Maybe there's a secret passageway right around here. And maybe Wishbone discovered some sign of it."

Wishbone jumped right out of Joe's arms, barking excitedly.

"But I don't see any secret passageway around here," David said, running his eyes over the rocks.

"That's exactly why it's a *secret* passageway!" Sam exclaimed.

Joe tugged at a few of the rocks that seemed to have interested Wishbone. Nothing happened. Then he tugged at a much larger rock. Surprisingly, it swung outward just a few inches.

"What's that?" David said, leaning forward and trying to see behind the rock.

Sam knelt down right beside the rock. She saw a little space between the rock and the hill. She reached in and found a thin metal bar. She lifted the metal bar, which seemed to be hooked into something.

"I think I just lifted some kind of a latch," Sam said. "Joe, give the rock another pull."

Both Joe and David tugged at the rock. This time the rock swung outward in David's hands. The three kids saw that the rock was attached to a movable iron frame that opened with the help of hinges. The rock was held in

place by tar and rope on the hidden side. The whole thing was a brilliantly disguised door.

"Sam, we'll never doubt you again," David said, studying the door with his sharp eyes. "It looks like this was made a long time ago."

Beyond the door lay a square opening that seemed large enough for a person to enter. The opening revealed only darkness.

Suddenly, Wishbone ran off into the darkness of the open doorway.

"Wishbone, come back!" Joe called.

Joe waited a moment, but Wishbone didn't return.

"I'd better go in after him," Joe said with annoyance. "There's no telling what's in there."

"All the more reason you *shouldn't* go in there," Sam pointed out.

"I've got to," Joe said, stooping over. "I'm not letting anything happen to Wishbone. I'll be right back."

Joe disappeared into the darkness.

"I can't let him go in there alone," David said, also stooping over.

David disappeared into the darkness.

Sam looked up toward Hathaway House. She saw no sign of Wanda coming with a flashlight. After a moment's thought, Sam decided to follow her friends into the mysterious opening. She figured they might need some help. Besides, she was eager to see what was in there. However, she told herself she wouldn't go too far, and she would keep listening for some sign of Wanda.

Stooping over, Sam stepped into the darkness.

Chapter Twenty

Wishbone moved through what was a pitch-dark tunnel. There was not a speck of light. The journey would have been impossible if it were not for the fact that the path was straight and empty.

The dog heard the distant footsteps of his friends. Aside from that, the tunnel was as silent as a tomb.

Where does this thing lead? Wishbone wondered.

"Wishbone!" the dog heard Joe call from a good distance behind. "Come here, boy!"

"Joe," Wishbone called back, "I've been calling *you* for the past twenty minutes, but you didn't come. Well, maybe you didn't hear me. But right now I really need to know where this tunnel leads—and I'm not stopping for anything or anybody—even you, buddy. This tunnel may very well have something to do with all the mysteries inside Hathaway House. Just keep following me. I'll make sure we'll be okay. I always do, don't I?"

There was no answer.

As Wishbone went along, he began to get a better

feel for the tunnel. It was roomy enough for a dog to walk through standing up, but Wishbone knew a regular-sized human would have to stoop. The walls, ceiling, and floor were covered with old boards that were partly rotted away. The whole place smelled of dirt and worms and dampness.

Wishbone could hear that his friends were gaining ground on him. Joe was no longer calling for him. Wishbone was sure that Joe, Sam, and David had become just as interested in the tunnel as he was. Soon Wishbone overheard the kids talking among themselves.

"So you really think that Josiah Hathaway used this tunnel?" Joe asked.

"That must be the answer," Sam replied. "I bet the tunnel goes right up to the house."

"I'm really impressed with this tunnel," David said. "It couldn't have been easy to build, especially not back in Josiah Hathaway's time. And he would have had to build the tunnel without anyone seeing it done."

Josiah Hathaway probably hired a few dogs to help out, Wishbone thought as he clicked his way onward. *When it comes to digging, dogs are world-class champs.*

"I knew it the first time I saw his portrait," Sam said. "Josiah Hathaway was one sneaky person."

Wishbone slowed down, hearing a new set of footsteps. Those footsteps weren't coming from behind him. They were coming from up ahead.

Wishbone stopped dead in his tracks.

Whoa! Who could that be?

Wishbone listened to the steady clip-clop of the approaching footsteps. The feet moved at a steady pace with confidence, as if they were very familiar with the tunnel.

"Do you hear something?" David asked his friends.

"Yeah, I think I do," Joe replied. "It sounds like footsteps coming from way up ahead. That couldn't be Miss Gilmore, could it?"

"I don't see how Miss Gilmore could be coming toward us from the direction of the house," Sam said nervously.

Wishbone could hear that Joe, Sam, and David had also stopped walking.

The tunnel was totally silent, except for the clip-clop of the mystery footsteps. Wishbone's fur bristled with alarm. With every approaching footstep, Wishbone's heartbeat seemed to be racing faster.

I hope I haven't gotten me and my friends into a real fix. If this person turns out to be dangerous, it might not be so easy to get out of here. And who knows if it's even a person? It could be a demon . . . or the ghost of Josiah Hathaway . . . or a giant mole monster or a . . .

"Who goes there?" Joe called out.

"Who goes *there?*" a strange voice called back.

"My name is . . . uh . . . Joe Talbot," Joe answered with hesitation. "I'm here with my friends Sam and David. My dog is here, too. Who are you?"

"I'll be right there," the mysterious voice called, moving ever closer. "Please do not be afraid. You have nothing to fear."

Wishbone waited, tensely, not moving a muscle.

Moments later, the footsteps came to a stop.

Wishbone just barely made out the silhouette of a human standing, or rather stooping, just a few feet away. The shadowy shape gave off the strong scent of Bay Rum.

"Who are you?" Sam whispered.

213

"I may cause you a bit of a shock," the voice replied. "Please remember, you have nothing to fear."

Wishbone raised his ears. He heard quickly moving footsteps coming from behind. It smelled like Wanda. Suddenly, a beam of bright light shot over the Jack Russell terrier's head, landing on the face of the unknown person.

It was an old man with blue eyes and a head of messed-up white hair. He wore a dirty flannel shirt. The man looked extremely familiar.

"Mr. Whipple?" Joe said with amazement.

Yeah—that's who this is! Oliver Matheson Whipple III. The lawyer who visited Wanda in Oakdale a few days ago. The last time I saw him, he was dressed in a suit and he had a moustache, but that's definitely him. I know that lawyers can do sneaky things, but what's this guy doing sneaking around in a secret tunnel?

The man held up a hand, shielding the flashlight's glare. "Uh . . . yes . . . I am Oliver Matheson Whipple the Third. But, well . . . that's not exactly who I am. . . . Is Miss Gilmore here also?"

"You bet I am," Wanda said firmly.

"Are you by any chance a relative of Homer Hathaway's?" Sam asked Mr. Whipple.

"In a way, I am a relative of his," Whipple admitted. "A very close relative."

"You've been trying to scare us," David said bravely. "You were angry that Wanda, not you, got Hathaway House. Isn't that right?"

"I'm afraid that's not exactly correct," Whipple said, his eyes squinting in the harsh light. "I suggest that we go back to the house and I will explain everything. The easiest way is to go back the way you folks came in. Let's head in that direction."

"How do we know that we can trust you?" Wanda said with suspicion.

"Suppose I go first," Whipple suggested. "That way you can keep your eyes on me. Does that sound fair?"

"Okay, you go first," Wanda said.

The man eased past the others, moving to the front of the line. He began leading the way out of the tunnel. Wanda kept the flashlight beam aimed on the man's back. The others followed, each of them stooped over, with Wishbone acting as the rear guard.

"Let me tell you once again," the man called back, "you folks have nothing to fear."

The more he says that, the more I don't believe it! Wishbone thought.

Chapter Twenty-one

Sam felt far from safe in Mr. Whipple's presence. She didn't trust the elderly fellow at all. Sam and her friends were all seated in the parlor with Mr. Whipple. The night's fire had almost died out, but a few scraps of wood still burned with a dim, red glow.

Mr. Whipple's flannel shirt and blue jeans were smeared with grime, and the man's snow-white hair was unbrushed. All the Oakdale visitors stared at Whipple, waiting impatiently for some truthful answers.

"I shall begin by first apologizing for what I put you through. I am very sorry. Next I want to tell you who I really am," Mr. Whipple said, calmly crossing his legs. "I am not Oliver Matheson Whipple the Third. In truth, I am . . . Homer Hathaway."

Wanda wrinkled her brow. "You *can't* be Homer Hathaway."

"He's *dead*," Sam said.

"He died in a sailing accident," Joe said.

"Somewhere in Greece," David added.

Wishbone gave his muzzle a confused shake.

"You only think Homer died because I told you so," Whipple said with a faint smile.

"But other people in town seem to think that he's dead," Wanda pointed out.

"Never mind about that," Whipple said with a wave of his hand. "I can assure you that I am none other than Homer Hathaway. I ought to know. I have been Homer Hathaway for the past eighty-four years."

Wanda tilted her head, studying the man's face. "Maybe you are Homer Hathaway. I did meet you once, many years ago. And I have seen a few photographs of you since then."

Sam noticed that the man's eyes were the same color of blue as Josiah Hathaway's eyes. She saw other similar features, too. These were all possible signs that the man was indeed a member of the Hathaway family, perhaps even Homer.

"As Oliver Matheson Whipple the Third," the man explained, "I wore a fake moustache and dressed much nicer than I normally do. This was to throw you off the track, Miss Gilmore, in case I looked too familiar to you."

Sam realized that the man in front of her didn't have any trace of Mr. Whipple's prim and proper personality. He seemed to be much more casual now.

"Then where's the real Oliver Whipple?" David asked.

For a brief moment, Sam wondered if this man had killed Oliver Whipple and hidden his body somewhere, maybe even in the house.

"There is no Oliver Whipple," the man said. "He's nothing but a product of my imagination."

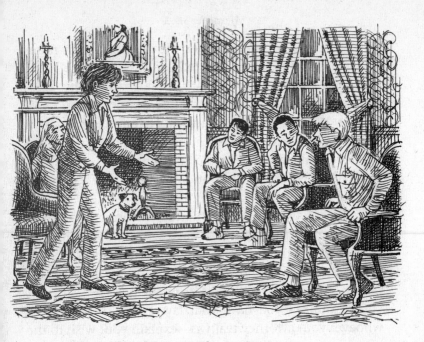

"I'm confused," Joe said.

"Very confused," David agreed.

Wanda shot to her feet, scowling at the man. "Is this some kind of a twisted, sick game? Have you been trying to scare us just for the fun of it? If that's the case, Mr. Whipple . . . I mean Mr. Hathaway . . . well, then, I'll have you know that I am very angry!"

From his spot on the floor, Wishbone released a low growl.

The man who had been claiming to be Homer Hathaway gave a patient nod. "I completely understand your anger. However, please take a few moments to hear me out. If you're still angry after you hear my story, then you can scream and shout at me all you want."

"Okay. Go ahead and start talking," Wanda said, returning to her seat.

It seemed to Sam as if even the portraits in the room were watching Homer, eager to hear his story.

"I'm in very good health for a man of my age," Homer Hathaway explained. "Still, I know I won't live forever. When I die, I want to will Hathaway House to a relative. The place has been in the family a long time, and I believe that tradition should continue."

"Well, that's understandable," Wanda said, still scowling.

"However," Homer Hathaway continued, "I'm not very close to the relatives I have left. I was afraid that whoever I left the house to might end up selling it. And, of course, once the house belongs to someone else, that person is free to do with it as he or she pleases."

"Couldn't you have your lawyer, Mr. Whipple—or whoever your attorney really is—explain your wish to the person who would inherit the house?" Wanda said. "The lawyer could make it clear—in writing, if necessary—you didn't want the house sold."

"Even so, I still feared the person would sell the house. Maybe not right away, but eventually."

"Why?"

"Because the house really is haunted," Homer said matter-of-factly. "At least I believe it is. Most of the ghostly happenings you folks encountered were faked. But not all of them."

"Which ones were real?" Sam asked.

"The doors opening and closing by themselves," Homer said, a lively twinkle appearing in his eyes. "They've been doing that for years. This may be due to natural causes. A small river runs deep underground, beneath this house. And the river may create enough disturbance in the earth so that it can cause the doors to react as they do. However, I believe that the doors are being opened and closed by a genuine ghost—or perhaps even several of them."

"At the very least, what happens with the doors makes it *seem* like the house is haunted," Joe said. "If you add that together with the rumors about the house, people might *think* the house is haunted—even if it's not."

Sam nodded. "The first time I saw one of the doors move, I thought a ghost had done it."

"Exactly," Hathaway said, pointing a finger in the air. "And most people don't like living in a house that is, or seems to be, haunted. That's why I was afraid someone would end up selling the house."

"Couldn't you just have met with me and explained the situation?" Wanda asked.

"Yes, I could have," Hathaway said in a reasonable tone. "But here's the problem. You might have told me 'Yes, I want the house, and, no, I won't sell it for any reason.' Then I die, and you take over the house. Sooner or later, even though you've been warned about the doors, they might start upsetting you. So you change your mind and put the house up for sale. And if you happened to be a little short on cash, this would make the idea of selling the house very tempting. By this time, I'll be dead and helpless to do anything about it."

Despite all the trickery, Sam found herself liking Homer Hathaway. She sympathized with his desire to protect the family home.

"Yes, I see your point," Wanda told Homer. "You felt you couldn't be sure about me, or any of the other relatives you have left."

"In other words," Homer stated, "I needed to will the house to a relative who would not be afraid of a little haunting."

"I see," Wanda said slowly. "So this whole setup was a test."

Sam remembered the words of Oliver Whipple. Back in Oakdale, he had said, "Miss Gilmore, it is you who will be testing the house. The house will not be testing you." As it turned out, this was not entirely true.

"Yes," Homer told Wanda. "I was testing you. I needed to convince you that the house was really haunted. Then, if you could handle the haunting with grace, humor, bravery, and compassion, I'd know you would be the perfect person to inherit Hathaway House!"

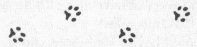

Wishbone was getting that dizzy feeling he got after chasing his tail for a few minutes. *Okay, let me get this straight. Homer Hathaway was afraid Wanda would be afraid of the ghosts in the house. So he invented a bunch of fake ghosts to see if she could handle being afraid of the ghosts. That makes sense . . . I guess.*

"I understand the reason behind your plan, Mr. Hathaway," Wanda said, no longer scowling at the man. "All the same, it seems extreme."

Joe said, "Mr. Hathaway, your prank went way past the practical-joke stage."

"I'll say it did," Wishbone added. "Dogs like me, we can take care of ourselves pretty well. But humans get very nervous about these things."

"Believe me, I realize my scheme was upsetting to all

of you," Homer admitted. "I was glad you didn't come to the house alone, Miss Gilmore. But then I was also concerned about frightening these three youngsters."

"What about the dog?" Wishbone asked, slightly offended. "Dogs have feelings, too, you know. But I'll have you know that I wasn't scared for even a single second."

"But you scared us, anyway," Sam pointed out.

Sadness entered Homer's eyes. "Please understand, it was very important to me that the house remain just as it is. I felt a family member, the right one, would be the most protective of the house. If the house went to the wrong family member, or some outsider, who knows? Hathaway House might be remodeled or even torn down. Things change so quickly in this world. Beautiful neighborhoods are turned into shopping malls. Books are replaced by video games. The list goes on and on. At the very least, I think a few things, such as this house, should stay the way they were always meant to be."

"I completely agree with you about that," Wanda said sympathetically.

"Though I tried," Homer continued, "I couldn't think of any other way to make sure I would be giving the house to the right person. My plan was the only foolproof method I could come up with. I tried to make the hauntings more playful than terrifying. Even so, some degree of fear was necessary to make the test work."

"I guess you're right about that," David said. "If Miss Gilmore could handle your 'ghosts,' then she could certainly handle the real ghosts. After all, they just open and close doors."

"It also wasn't very nice of you to let your friends think you were dead," Sam told Homer.

"Actually, I told my closest friends about my plan. The others really do think I'm dead. It'll probably give some of them a good scare when they see me out and about tomorrow morning."

"I know some lobster fishermen I wouldn't mind giving a scare to," Wishbone told the old man.

"Teddy Lyman is one of my closest friends," Homer said. "He was actually in on the scheme with me. I told him to pretend he was interested in buying the house. He was supposed to pressure you, Miss Gilmore, for an answer by tomorrow morning, after you had spent three nights in the haunted house. If, at that time, you agreed to sell the house . . . or even seemed close to it . . . then you would have failed the test. I'd know there was a good chance that you would sell the house somewhere down the line."

"And then you would have put another relative to the test?" Wanda asked.

"Yes. But I very much hoped you'd pass the test, Miss Gilmore. I remembered you very well from that time when I met you many years ago. I liked you the very instant we met."

"I liked you, too, Mr. Hathaway."

"Please, call me Homer," Homer said, showing a very friendly smile.

Wanda returned the smile. "And you may call me Wanda."

"I'm so glad everybody likes everybody," Wishbone said with a wag of his tail. "What do you say we celebrate with a very early morning snack?"

Homer didn't seem to hear the suggestion.

Wishbone shifted from a sitting position into a

lying-down position. He was near the fireplace on the Oriental rug, which had become his favorite spot in the house. After so many years of use, the rug had been broken in just right.

"For years," Homer said after a weary sigh, "I've put off making out a will because I found the whole idea very unpleasant. Finally, my lawyer convinced me I needed to do it. I came up with a list of relatives and then contacted my first choice, which was you, Wanda."

"How did you know what I'd be like?" Wanda asked. "You hadn't seen me since I was seven years old."

Homer's eyes twinkled with mischief. "That's the real reason I came, as Mr. Whipple, to see you in person. I wanted to make sure you were still the spirited and spunky person I remembered. And you certainly are."

"When did you plan all the details about the hauntings?" David asked.

"I started around four weeks before I came to Oakdale. I let the house get dusty so it would look as if Homer Hathaway had been away for some time. I put the sheets over the furniture the very morning you folks arrived at the house."

Wanda shook her head with disbelief. "This test is the craziest thing I've ever heard of."

"I know it's crazy," Homer said, looking closely at Wanda. "But now that you understand the reason behind it, are you still angry with me?"

"I ought to be," Wanda said firmly, meeting Homer's eyes. "Maybe I'm just as crazy as you are, though, because I think I understand. No, I suppose I'm not really angry with you, Homer. But let me ask you something. Did I pass the test?"

"The test ended early because . . . well, a few things went wrong here tonight," Homer explained. "And yet, that's not a problem. I'll tell you why. In the middle of the séance a few hours back, Wanda, you cried out the following words to the ghosts: 'If I keep this house, all of you ghosts will be welcome here anytime you like!' At that moment, I knew that you were a person who could welcome the ghosts of Hathaway House with open arms."

Wanda frowned, as if remembering something. "I guess I did say that, didn't I?"

"It was a wonderful moment," Homer said, touching his chest. "It brought tears to my eyes. Yes, Wanda, you've passed my test with flying colors. I offer you my congratulations! The house will be yours—if you really want it, that is."

"Well, let me make sure I have this right," Wanda said. "The only thing that might really be ghostly activity is the opening and closing of the doors?"

"Oh, I've seen and heard a few other little things over the years. But they're very minor."

"Yes, Homer," Wanda said with a big nod, "I am absolutely certain that I want the house."

Wishbone's ears crept upward, hearing something. He whipped his muzzle around toward the study door, which was wide open.

The study was dark, but Wishbone could see that a section of the bookcase was swinging outward, almost as if it were a door. When the bookcase was open all the way, Wishbone saw the silhouette of a human figure appear.

Here we go again!

Wishbone barked loudly, springing to his four feet.

226

Chapter Twenty-two

At the sound of Wishbone's bark, everyone looked around in confusion.

The Jack Russell terrier was fully prepared to defend his pack. Wishbone watched the shadowy figure move through the darkness of the study. No one said a single word as the figure stepped through the study doorway, entering the parlor.

Wishbone could see that it was an elderly lady, dressed casually in a sweater and pants. The lady's gray hair wasn't tied up neatly at the back, she didn't wear glasses, and she didn't seem at all like a schoolteacher. Otherwise, she looked almost exactly like Miss Bridgewater, the ghost investigator.

The dog turned to his friends, all of whom seemed as shocked as himself.

"Do not be alarmed," the lady said calmly. "It is only I, Miss Isabella Bridgewater."

"What are you doing here?" Homer said, sounding only mildly surprised.

The lady held up an insulated container. "I came to bring you some hot coffee, Homer."

"This whole situation just keeps getting stranger and stranger," Wishbone muttered to himself.

"For a moment there, I thought I was understanding everything," Sam said. "Now I'm confused all over again."

Homer smiled at the woman. "This attractive lady isn't really Miss Bridgewater. She is, in fact, Blanche Pratt, of Jellymore, New Hampshire. That's a little town about nine miles northwest of here. Blanche is a friend of mine."

"Actually, I'm his girlfriend," the woman said, as she took a seat near Homer.

"Girlfriend?" Wishbone whispered to Joe.

"Girlfriend?" David said with amazement.

Homer turned his blue eyes on David. "Yes, girlfriend, young man."

Wishbone settled back onto his Oriental rug, ready to hear more explanations.

"Were you in on the scheme, too, Miss Bridgewater?" Wanda asked.

"It's Miss Pratt," the lady said, pouring some coffee into the container's cuplike top. "But, please, call me Blanche. And, yes, I'm afraid I was in on the scheme. Let me say from the start, though, that I thought it was a ridiculous idea. But when Homer gets his mind set on something, he's as stubborn as a mule. Finally, I saw how much it meant to Homer to get the right owner for the house. So I lent a hand."

Blanche was much more casual than Miss Bridgewater had been. Wishbone even got the feeling that this lady might be a good "chase the stick" partner.

"Say, Blanche," Wishbone said politely, "you didn't happen to bring any cookies along with that coffee, did you?"

Blanche didn't seem to hear the question.

"Are you really a parapsychologist Miss Bridgewater, I mean Miss Pratt?" Joe asked.

"Heavens, no," Blanche replied. "I own a small pottery store. But most of the information I gave you about ghosts is true."

"I prepared her well for her role," Homer said, after a sip of coffee. "Myself, I've had an interest in ghosts for most of my life. I've read all sorts of books on the subject. I've even had a few ghost investigators and mediums come out here to the house."

"Did they think the house was haunted?" Sam asked.

Homer shrugged. "Some did, some didn't."

"All that silly equipment Miss Bridgewater brought with her belongs to Homer," Blanche said with a scoff.

"I have to hand it to you, Miss Pratt," David said. "You certainly played your part well."

"Why, thank you," Blanche said with a charming smile.

"She's a fine amateur actress," Homer said, patting Blanche's hand. "She recently performed one of the leading roles in the Jellymore Community Theater production of *Arsenic and Old Lace.* She played this very sweet lady who invites trusting men to her house and then poisons and kills them and buries them in her basement. Blanche was really charming in the role."

"Oh, Blanche, may I ask you something?" Wanda said, waving an arm for attention. "Why did you come out of the bookcase just now?"

I was just about to ask her the same thing, Wishbone thought.

"After the séance earlier tonight," Blanche explained, "Homer and I decided we would do no more fake haunting. But Homer didn't want to make himself known to you until after tonight, just in case you changed your mind about keeping the house for yourself."

"Blanche went home," Homer continued, "but she insisted I stay in the house for a few hours. She wanted me to make sure no one became too frightened. She could see that Sam was really shaken up by seeing my hands come through the floor."

Blanche frowned at Homer. "And that happened only because of your foolishness."

"You folks seemed to be doing all right in the house," Homer continued. "So I decided to leave a short while back. I must have entered the tunnel from the house side right about the same time you folks entered the tunnel from the bay side."

"And I entered the house through the tunnel just a few minutes ago," Blanche said. "I figured Homer might need some hot coffee. I didn't know how long he was going to be here, and I didn't want him falling asleep on the job. I came through the bookcase when I overheard all of you talking in the parlor. The bookcase is the only way there is to get into the main part of the house from the tunnel."

"Tell me," Homer said, scratching at his white hair, "how in the world did you folks discover that tunnel?"

Sam explained the series of events that led to her and her friends finding the tunnel. When she was done, Homer confirmed that Sam had been absolutely right about Josiah Hathaway using the tunnel to smuggle some of his goods from his ships to his house.

However, Homer explained that Josiah Hathaway hadn't been the one who had built the tunnel. It had been built when Josiah was just a boy. During the Revolutionary War, the Americans had used the tunnel to hide supplies from the attacking British army. Josiah knew about the tunnel and made it a point to build his house right near it.

"That tunnel is so well disguised, nobody ever stumbles onto it," Homer told the group. "And the Hathaways have always done their best to keep it a complete secret. After almost two hundred years, we're still quite embarrassed that our ancestor cheated on his taxes."

"I'd say some of that sneakiness still runs in the family," Wanda said, staring at Homer.

"Oh, ho-ho!" Blanche said with a loud laugh. "You have got that right!"

"Where did Josiah Hathaway hide his smuggled goods?" Sam asked. "In the basement?"

"No, no, no, Josiah was even sneakier than that," Homer said with a glint in his eye. "Many times, the customs inspectors came to check the basement, but they never found a thing. I'll show you exactly how the sly fox pulled off his scheme."

Homer got up and motioned for the others to follow him. He led the group to the opened bookcase in the study. As Wishbone peered into the opening, Wanda aimed her flashlight beam inside it.

A hollow area extended about four feet from the wall. The hollow area, which was very dark, extended both upward and downward. The place was almost as damp and musty as the basement had been.

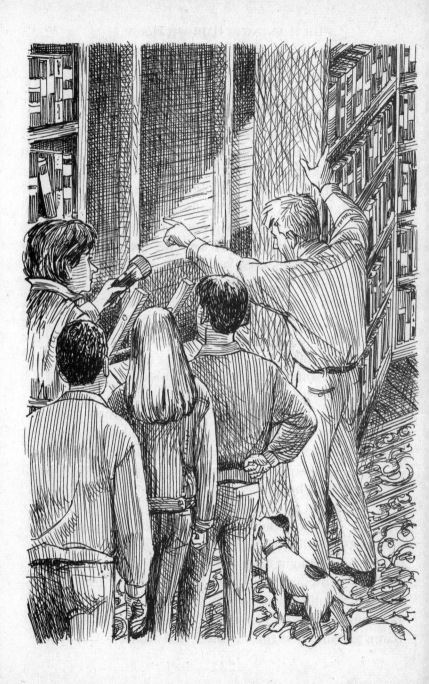

"When Josiah had the house built back in 1819, he had something very specific in mind," Homer explained. "He told the carpenters to build a secret storage area. The entire south wall of the house is a false wall, as is part of the western wall. Behind the false walls, there is a hollow area that runs from the basement to the top floor. That's what you're looking at now."

"The tunnel leads right down there at the basement level," Blanche said, pointing downward. "The cargo was brought there. Then it could be taken to different levels throughout the hollow storage area. On every floor, there is a wooden platform on which the cargo could be placed. The cargo could be moved up and down by a type of elevator system."

"The elevator must have worked by a system of ropes and pulleys," David said.

"That's correct," Homer said. "The ropes and pulleys no longer work. But a person can climb from floor to floor because there's also a ladder back there."

"When Josiah was ready to sell the hidden cargo," Blanche added, "he would bring it out through this large opening behind the bookcase."

Wishbone stole a glance at the portrait of Josiah Hathaway. *You know, pal, you are sneakier than a squirrel storing away its acorns for the winter.*

"But wait, there's more," Homer said, stepping through the opening.

As if by magic, Homer disappeared into the darkness. Moments later, Wishbone heard him calling from the next room.

Wishbone and the others hurried back into the parlor. Homer's head was sticking through a trapdoor that was on the floor right beneath the portrait of Lydia Hathaway. That was where Sam had seen the hands.

Homer gave a playful grin. "Throughout the house, there are these little trapdoors. If you're standing in the room, these doors can't be opened, or indeed, even seen. They can be opened only from the secret side."

"What are they for?" Sam asked.

"Air and light," Homer replied. "Remember, air conditioning and electric lighting didn't exist back then. I keep a bunch of flashlights back here, but usually I don't need them. I've been climbing around in these walls since I was just a child."

And you're still doing it, Wishbone thought.

"Are there trapdoors in every room?" Joe asked.

"Only the rooms on the southern half of the house," Homer said. "That includes the parlor, the study, and the bedrooms that are being used by Joe and Sam."

"The tunnel allowed Homer and me to get in and out of the house unnoticed," Blanche explained. "The storage area allowed us to move around the house. The trapdoors helped us carry out many of our ghostly tricks."

Wishbone gave his side a scratch. *Hmm . . . these trapdoors could be very useful for stashing away some forbidden snacks. If Wanda ends up with this house, I'll have to give it a try.*

Homer came back into the parlor, through the bookcase opening, and everyone returned to their seats. Sam saw Wishbone settle down comfortably onto his favorite Oriental rug. From the storage area, Homer had brought a suitcase, which Sam quickly recognized as Miss Bridge-water's suitcase.

Sam was still tickled by the fact that Homer and Blanche were actually boyfriend and girlfriend. Homer and Blanche had such a youthful spirit about them that they didn't seem so much older than Sam herself.

Homer flashed a grin. "Now, do you want to know how we pulled off all of the haunting incidents?"

"Homer, I'm sure they want to know *everything*," Blanche said flatly.

"The whole scheme worked very much like a three-act play," Homer said, obviously proud of his plan. "On Friday afternoon, Blanche and I watched you from a distance as you arrived. We could see exactly who would be staying in the house. Around ten o'clock Friday night, Blanche and I entered the house through the tunnel. It was almost time for the first round of haunting."

"It had to be Joe and Sam who experienced the first hauntings," Blanche said. "That's because they were the only ones in rooms with false walls."

Homer opened the suitcase and pulled out a small white device with fan blades. "I went first. I was hiding behind the false wall in Sam's room. I opened the trap-door and saw that Sam was reading in bed. I was holding this battery-powered fan. It's very powerful, but almost totally silent. I aimed the fan at the wind chimes, turned it on, and—presto!—the wind chimes began to move. Naturally, Sam stared at the wind chimes a few moments. While she did that, I reached through the trap-door, then wound and opened the music box. By the time Sam looked at the playing music box, I had already closed the trapdoor."

"Oh, I see," Sam said, nodding.

"A lot of our tricks used the magician's method of 'misdirection,'" Homer explained. "Simply put, this means you get the audience to look at one thing, such as the wind chimes, while you are fiddling with something else, such as the music box."

"But I didn't notice any haunting in my room," Joe said, looking puzzled.

Blanche pulled a rubber ball from the suitcase. "Your haunting was simpler, Joe. It had to be, because the trap-door in your room has become too difficult to open. All I did was bounce this ball for a few moments. But you were sleeping so soundly you didn't notice it. That's why Sam was the only one who experienced a haunting the first night."

Wishbone lifted his head, as if he disagreed with something being said.

"The following night, I tinkered with the wind chimes and music box again in Sam's room," Homer said. "Joe's room didn't get haunted that night because Miss Bridgewater was spending the night in the house. I hope she didn't bother anyone with her snoring."

"I don't snore," Blanche argued.

"Oh, you do, too," Homer replied.

"But we're getting a bit ahead of ourselves," Wanda interrupted. "What about Saturday morning? How did the water boil so quickly?"

"After Blanche and I had completed our haunting on Friday night," Homer said, "I came into the main part of the house through the bookcase. I sprinkled some harmless powdered chemicals into the teakettle. The chemicals are what caused the water to boil so fast. As the

236

water boiled, all traces of the chemicals disappeared. I got the chemicals and the idea from a friend of mine who works in the science field."

"Homer was especially proud of that trick," Blanche told the group.

"It really stumped us," Joe admitted.

"And this brings us to Act Two of our ghostly play," Homer said, rubbing his hands together with enthusiasm. "This was the act that started 'Miss Bridgewater.' She was quite necessary to the plot. You see, it was important that the four of you believe that the house had a ghost, not just a prankster. The whole purpose of Miss Bridgewater was to convince you that the house really was haunted."

"And it worked," David said. "Even on me."

"Miss Bridgewater's first trick was to slip more of the powdery chemical into the teakettle," Blanche said. "I did this while I was pretending to check the kettle. That's why the water boiled so fast the second time."

"You're pretty clever yourself," Sam told Blanche.

"Now, tell us all about the ghost investigation in the parlor," Wanda said. "There were all kinds of interesting things going on in there."

Homer pulled a perfume bottle out of the suitcase. "While all of you were in the dining room with Miss Bridgewater, I opened one of the parlor trapdoors. I sprayed a bit of this lavender perfume into the room, blew it outward with the fan, then closed the trapdoor. Wishbone smelled the perfume first and led you into the room."

"What about the temperature reading?" Joe asked.

Homer pulled out a spray can and a thin rubber hose. "I went to the parlor's other trapdoor, opened it, then sprayed some of this chemical into the room. The chemical is a coolant. It's used in many air conditioners and refrigerators. For a brief time, the chemical cooled a small section of the room. So the temperature drop showed on the thermal scanner."

"What about the EMF reading?" David asked.

Homer pulled out a device that resembled a TV remote control. "This is a radio transmitter that I got from my scientist friend. Once again, I opened the trapdoor. Then I aimed this thing at the EMF detector. The radio waves from the transmitter made the EMF dial show a decent level of electromagnetism."

"But Miss Bridgewater told me to keep a careful watch on the room," Wanda said, looking confused. "Wasn't there a chance that I would see the trapdoor opening?"

"Even though I told you to watch the room," Blanche said, "I fooled you into missing the trapdoor. I was simply using more misdirection. I also had to make sure I was talking while the chemical was being sprayed, because it makes a hissing noise."

Sam remembered how Miss Bridgewater had directed the attention of the group. Whenever she moved somewhere or pointed at something, everyone looked in that direction.

"What about the photograph with the ghostly face?" Sam asked. "I took that picture myself, and David is the one who put the disk into the computer."

"That was the trick that really got me believing in a ghost," David said. "How could you have faked that?"

"This one was my idea," Blanche said, as she pulled two floppy disks out of the suitcase. "After the ghost investigation, Sam handed me the floppy disk that contained the photos she had taken. I headed for the entrance hall, on my way to get the laptop out of my car. But then David stopped me, saying he wanted to use his own laptop. I returned to the parlor. But, by that time, I had switched Sam's floppy disk for another one that looked just like it. See, here are the two disks."

"Ahhhh," Joe said, suddenly understanding. "So we weren't looking at the pictures Sam took."

"No, you were looking at pictures that I had already taken," Blanche said. "Remember, Sam took pictures in a dark room with no flash. That made it impossible to tell the difference between her photographs and mine. Except, I had a ghostly image on one of my photographs. My nephew is an absolute expert with computers, and he did it for me."

"You guys are so good it's scary," Sam commented.

"Thanks," Homer and Blanche said together.

"What about the séance?" Wanda asked.

"Yes, the séance," Homer said excitedly. "Our third and final act."

"In the early evening today," Blanche said, "we heard you folks plan to have a séance. You see, off and on we were hiding behind the false walls, listening to your conversations. Miss Bridgewater, of course, had encouraged the idea of the séance."

"We decided to give you a gala of ghosts," Homer said with a dramatic gesture. "By that time, we had made believers of all of you, and we felt sure we could pull off the scheme. In honor of Wishbone, we even threw in a ghostly canine."

Sam already knew how the pair had produced the perfume smell. But Homer and Blanche pulled various items out of the suitcase, showing how they had produced all the ghostly noises. They used the rubber ball, a set of wind chimes, a blackboard and chalk, and a dog's squeak toy. The kettle whistle had been created with a bosun's whistle, an item used on sailboats. Homer had given all the ghostly knocks by knocking on the secret side of the wall with his fist.

"We were really busy with our special effects," Homer said, as he and Blanche put the items back into the suitcase. "But I could tell that all of you were enjoying the show. It was around this time that I heard Wanda cry out, 'If I keep this house, all of you ghosts will be welcome here anytime you like!'"

"What about the hands by the wall?" Sam asked.

Blanche glared at her boyfriend. "Homer tried to go too far with his trickery, and he got caught."

"It's true," Homer said with embarrassment. "A few hours earlier, I had overheard Sam telling Wanda about her Lydia Hathaway theory. I liked the theory very much. So when Wanda asked why the ghosts felt so welcome in the house, I opened the trapdoor and tilted Lydia's portrait. But I got caught red-handed."

"And the curtain quickly came down on our ghostly play," Blanche said, still glaring at Homer.

"But it was a great show," Joe said, smiling. "People pay money to tour haunted houses on Halloween, but I bet no one has gotten anything like this performance."

Feeling a slight swish of air, Sam turned toward the study. She saw the study door closing—slowly, silently, all by itself. The others noticed it, too.

"But you two had nothing to do with the doors opening and closing," Wanda said, staring at the door.

"Isn't that what you told us, Homer?"

"No, no, nothing at all," Homer said with a pleased expression.

Blanche rolled her eyes. "Homer believes the doors are opened and closed by real ghosts."

"They are," Homer insisted.

"They are not."

"They are."

"They are not."

"Blanche and I have different views on this topic," Homer told the others.

Wanda smiled. "Even so, the two of you make quite a lovely couple."

"About a year ago," Homer said, patting Blanche's knee, "my church and her church had a social for singles. Just as I was pouring some punch into my glass, I laid eyes on this magnificent woman. Well, I was so taken, I dropped my glass into the punch bowl."

"He was the cutest thing," Blanche said, pinching Homer's chin. "When I first talked with him, he was as tongue-tied as a teenager. I took a liking to him right away."

"You certainly did not," Homer argued.

"I did, too."

"You did not."

"I did, too!"

"It seems you two share differing views on a lot of topics," David said with a chuckle.

"Do you two have any plans to get married?" Wanda asked.

Blanche gave Homer a look of fake annoyance. "Oh, we've been talking about it. But Homer, here, is afraid of commitment. Typical man!"

It was a good three minutes before Sam, Joe, David, and Wanda stopped laughing.

These people are too much, Sam thought with amusement. *They're old enough to be my grandparents, and yet they're as full of fun as a couple of kids. I hope they end up getting married. They're perfect for each other!*

At the moment, Sam felt completely happy in Hathaway House. The furnishings were well over a century in age. The house had been built by a man who had cheated on his taxes. There was a chance that the house was truly haunted. But even so, Sam felt as if the time-worn walls were surrounding her with friendship, warmth, and hope.

"Let me ask you this," Sam told Homer. "If the house *is* really haunted, who do you think the ghost might be?"

"I've done a lot of research on the Hathaway family," Homer said. "But I still don't have the foggiest idea who the ghost is. The Hope Hathaway theory is a possibility, but there isn't a shred of evidence that she was really murdered. I seriously doubt that she was."

"But you like my theory about Lydia Hathaway?" Sam said, looking at Lydia's portrait.

Homer's eyes lit up with a lively twinkle. "The truth is, I do like your theory about my great-aunt Lydia. In fact, from now on, that is what I will choose to believe. I'll just believe that she was such a wonderful hostess she extended her hospitality to all the ghosts in the graveyard. As a result, they come romp around the house anytime they please."

Sam glanced at the fireplace. There was nothing left there except a chunk of a single log, its surface charred to an ashy gray. Yet, somewhere inside the log, a spot of redness continued to glow with a fiery heat.

Blanche took hold of Homer's hand. "Wanda, I'm afraid Homer won't be leaving this world for a good long while. I won't permit it. I like him too much. But when he does go, as all of us must, the house will be yours. And I know that you, too, will be a most wonderful hostess."

"Now and for all time," Wanda announced, "everyone—and I mean *everyone*—will be welcome in Hathaway House!"

Chapter Twenty-three

MONDAY

Sam gazed at a house so old it made Hathaway House look fairly new. It had been built in 1668, more than a hundred years before the United States had even become a country.

Built in the clapboard style, the wooden exterior was colored a sinister grayish-black. Sections of the house stuck out here and there, as if the person who designed it couldn't decide which way it should face. Sam spent a few minutes walking around the house, counting the many gables that jutted out from the roof area. There were seven of them.

In fact, this was the very house that had inspired Nathaniel Hawthorne to write *The House of the Seven Gables*. It was located in Salem, Massachusetts, where Nathaniel Hawthorne had lived for much of his life. Since Salem was on the way to Boston, Wanda had decided to bring the group there for a brief visit, on the way back to the airport.

"People lived in this house until 1910," Wanda said,

looking at a guidebook. "Then it was turned into a tourist attraction. Let's see. . . . Oh, Nathaniel Hawthorne was familiar with the house because it belonged to a cousin of his."

Sam was standing beside Wanda, Joe, David, and Wishbone on a brick pathway that surrounded the house. A number of tourists were walking around the area, also looking at the historic house.

"Does it look as creepy as it seemed in the book?" David asked Sam.

"It sure does," Sam said, after snapping yet another picture. "But it's really neat to see a house that inspired a book I just read. Maybe that's the window where Clifford liked to watch the activity in the street. And maybe that's the room where Holgrave lived. Somewhere around there on the ground floor must have been where Hepzibah had

her penny shop. And there's the yard where Phoebe would visit with the chickens. Oh, and that must be the parlor where both Colonel Pyncheon and Judge Pyncheon died."

"There's a guided tour of the house," Wanda said, checking her watch. "I think we have time if you kids are interested. I've seen it before. I don't mind waiting outside with Wishbone."

"I don't know about that tour," Joe said jokingly. "This place looks pretty scary."

"After what we've been through," David said, "I don't think *anything* will scare us."

"I wouldn't be so sure of that," Sam said, heading for the house's entrance. "Let's do the tour, anyway."

Along with seven other people, Sam, Joe, and David spent an hour going through the house with a tour guide. The inside of the house was decorated and furnished very much like Hathaway House. Sam learned all sorts of interesting things about the house, including the fact that it had a secret passageway. A section of the wall opened up to reveal a narrow brick chamber, where a winding staircase led to the next floor.

In the parlor, Sam stood and admired a lovely oil portrait of Nathaniel Hawthorne as a young man. His youthful face was set off by flowing dark hair and the beautiful eyes of a dreamer.

After the tour, the Oakdale group headed back to where their car was parked. They passed a block of old clapboard houses in which families continued to live. Each historic house had a plaque that told when the house had been built.

As Sam glanced at the houses, she imagined Hathaway House. Her last glimpse of the house had been just when she and her friends had driven away from it, about three hours ago. Homer and Blanche had been standing in the doorway, smiling as they waved a farewell.

Homer had told Wanda, Sam, David, Joe, and Wishbone that they were welcome to come visit anytime they pleased. Sam, for one, was already thinking about making a return visit. She realized that she was going to miss Homer and Blanche, not to mention the ghosts . . . if they really existed.

Halloween was a big event in Salem, and the entire town was decorated. As the group neared the center of town, they saw that the street was lined with dangling skeletons, floating ghosts, flying witches, and hundreds of jack-o'-lanterns. A group of women walked by, each dressed in the typical black costume of a witch. Sam felt goose bumps rise on her arm, remembering that Salem was the home of the dreaded witch trials.

Just a few days ago, Sam thought with a smile, *Joe, David, and I figured we were too old for Halloween. Well, we were wrong about that. This turned out to be coolest Halloween of our lives. The tricks were scary beyond belief, and there were plenty of surprising treats along the way. All of us had a great time, including Wishbone and Wanda. I think Homer and Blanche had a great Halloween, too. For that matter, so did the ghosts . . . if they exist.*

Sam noticed a light spring in her step as she walked. Even though she was now a fifteen-year-old high-school student, she suddenly felt as if she were beginning her childhood all over again.

I've been so worried about growing up, but maybe it's not such a big problem. Sure, some things change, but maybe you never get too old to have yourself a thrilling Halloween experience. Even if you're ninety. Or . . . even if you're a ghost!

Wishbone stared at a Halloween scarecrow that hung from a lamppost. Its straw body was covered with old-fashioned clothing, and its head was made out of a gigantic pumpkin. The pumpkin had brightly colored leaves for hair, and it wore a terrifying smile made of corn-kernel teeth.

Wishbone noticed a shadow-black cat lurking near the scarecrow. The cat stopped and stared at Wishbone with its greenish-yellow eyes.

A shiver ran through Wishbone's fur.

I know most black cats look alike. But something about this cat's eyes makes me think it's the exact same cat I met in Endicott. Is that possible? If it is, how did it get here? Did it chase after our car? Did it ride a broomstick?

The cat kept staring at Wishbone as the dog walked by. Its hypnotic eyes seemed to say "Who knows where I will follow you next? Or who knows where you will follow me?"

Maybe it is a witch-cat, after all, Wishbone thought, as he stole a last glance at the cat. *I'm pretty sure those witches that were hanged in Salem weren't really witches, but . . . Well, this has been a really mysterious vacation.*

After the group went another block, they reached their rental car. Sam and Wishbone had a slight disagreement about who would get the left-window side of the backseat. They worked it out, though, deciding that Wishbone would sit in Sam's lap for a while.

Soon the group was back on the road.

Wishbone watched the brilliant colors of the New England leaves fly by. A gust of wind sent a flurry of leaves to the ground. Wishbone felt a little bad for the leaves, but he knew they would spend the winter months feeding the soil. That, in turn, would nourish the trees and help them to sprout brand-new leaves in the springtime.

Nature really has it all worked out, Wishbone thought with admiration.

Before long, the humans were playing the Ghost word game.

"W," Wanda said.

"R," Joe said.

"A," David said.

After a long pause, Sam said, "I."

"There's no word that starts with W-R-A-I," David said.

"Do you challenge me?" Sam asked.

"We challenge you," Joe said.

"W-R-A-I-T-H," Sam said proudly.

"Wraith?" Joe said with puzzlement. "What's that?"

"Aha!" Wanda cried out. *"Wraith* is another word for *ghost.* Excellent, Sam!"

Wishbone gave Sam a sloppy lick on the face. "No question about it, Sam. When it comes to Ghost, you're the champion!"

Wishbone turned to see a long stretch of the Atlantic Ocean out the window. The sun shone down on the water, highlighting the blueness here and there with patches of bright white. Waves rolled across the water's surface, turning into swells of foam as they broke upon a sandy beach. A seagull soared high in the sky, off to some unknown destination.

I'll be glad to get back to Oakdale, Wishbone thought, his tongue panting with happiness. *I miss all my hometown friends and foods. But I have to say, this was the most fun, most frightening, most fantastic Halloween of all time. But then, of course, who knows about next year? And the year after that. And the year after . . .*

The waves faded from view, but Wishbone knew they would just keep rolling across the water forever.

About Alexander Steele

Alexander Steele is a writer of books, plays, and screenplays for both juveniles and adults. And sometimes for dogs. He has written *Tale of the Missing Mascot, Case of the On-Line Alien, Case of the Unsolved Case,* and *Case of the Breaking Story* for the WISHBONE Mysteries series. He has written *Moby Dog* and *The Last of the Breed* for The Adventures of Wishbone series, and *Unleashed in Space* for The SUPER Adventures of Wishbone series.

Alexander has written a total of sixteen books for kids, covering such interesting subjects as pirate treasure, snow leopards, and radio astronomy. He is now in the process of creating a new series of juvenile books. It's about . . . well, he can't reveal what it's about yet. Among Alexander's plays is the award-winning *One Glorious Afternoon,* which features Shakespeare and his fellow players at the Globe Theatre.

One of Alexander's first writing projects was a stage adaptation of Nathaniel Hawthorne's *The Scarlet Letter.* The play never became the worldwide success that Alexander had hoped for—so he was glad to have another chance to work with Mr. Hawthorne. Alexander hopes the ghost of Nathaniel Hawthorne has the time to pick up a copy of *The Haunting of Hathaway House.* By the way, even though Alexander doesn't really believe in ghosts, he is terrified of them.

Alexander lives in New York City, in a historic neighborhood where many of the buildings are almost as old as Hathaway House.

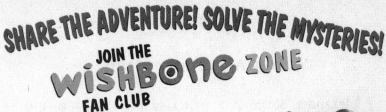